AWAY FROM KEYBOARD COLLECTION

DEFENDING HIS HOPE

PATRICIA D. EDDY

Cover Design: Deranged Doctor Design

Cover Photo: Paul Henry Serres

Proofreading: Book Dweller Proofreading

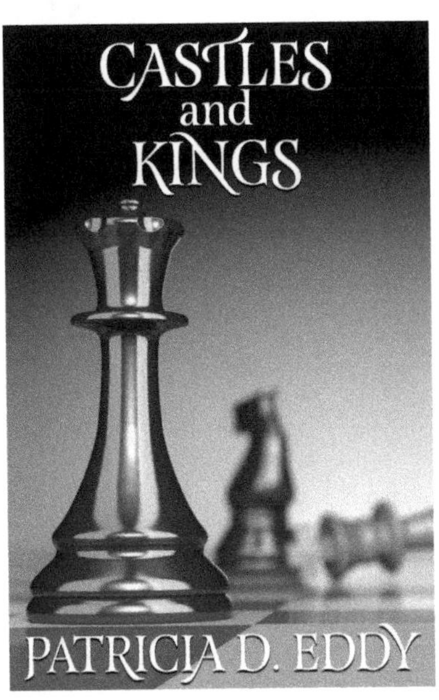

If you love sexy romantic suspense, I'd love to send you a short story set in Dublin, Ireland. Castles & Kings isn't available anywhere except for my mailing list. Click the link below and tell me where to send your free short story! http://patriciadeddy.com.

PROLOGUE

Four Years Ago

Wyatt

The desert winds whip over the desolate landscape as we make our way towards a cluster of buildings surrounded by a low stone wall. Four of us, moving as a single unit, stick to the shadows. The moon is nothing but a sliver in the darkened sky, and it's quiet except for the skittering of the scorpions along the hard-packed sand.

Giving the signal to breach, I adjust the grip on my M4. Intel says the group we're looking for is hiding in an underground tunnel accessible by a trap door in the corner of the main room.

Clearing the darkened space takes less than five seconds. It's empty save for a few discarded rags and a broken chair. Marklin draws down on the west wall, and my NVGs reveal the faint outline of a wooden panel set into the floor. We move together until Berlios drops to one knee.

A loud roar fills my ears. The blast of heat and flame overwhelms my senses, the light blinding me through the night-vision. Pain, sharp in some places, dull and aching in others, is the only way I can tell I'm still alive.

"Marklin!" I can't hear shit. Only a high-pitched whine. On my back, I rip off the NVGs and blink hard, waiting for the ceiling to come into focus. When it does...fuck. Half the roof is gone. So's the west wall.

Gritting my teeth, I roll to one side. A wave of agony races down my chest to my hip. Shit. There's a jagged piece of shrapnel poking out of my shoulder. Right where my radio should be.

Not good, Wyatt. Not good.

A rough grip to my wrist sends me scrambling for my rifle until I hear a familiar voice. "Gotta move. Now!" Berlios snaps. At least the ringing in my ears has faded. He crouches next to me, pulls my arm around his shoulders, and stands.

Jesus Fucking Christ, the pain is too much. My vision darkens and Berlios drags me from the house through a hole in the east wall. The door is completely gone.

Marklin and Hernandez stumble after us, and I try to turn my head. I have to make sure they're okay. Hernandez cradles his right arm, and his hand...his thick glove is gone, as is his thumb. Marklin's face is bloody, a dazed look in his eyes, but they're both moving under their own power. Thank God.

Someone knew we were coming. Knew the perfect time to blow the wall.

The world starts to spin, slowly at first, then faster, and the last thing I hear is Berlios calling my name. And then everything goes black.

Three Years Ago

The truck coasts to a stop over a carpet of moss and spring crocuses. From the back seat, Murphy, the dog who served by my side for most of my last two years in the SEALs, makes an inquisitive noise.

"You sure about this, Wyatt?" The man behind the wheel, West Sampson, shuts off the engine and peers at the cabin in front of us. "This place is in the middle of fucking nowhere."

"That's the point." The fresh air holds the promise of warmth, though it's still brisk enough I'll need to fire up the wood stove in the main room before dark. "I tried, West. For six months, I tried to find a way to deal with the noise. The traffic. The sirens. I can't do it anymore. I'll be better...out here."

Murphy stays close as West and I unload his truck. Everything I own in the world fits in three rucksacks and half a dozen boxes. "I'd ask if you wanted to come in, but..."

West huffs out a laugh. "You don't want company. I get it. I won't stay. You need me to run through the security system one more time before I head back to Seattle?"

"No. I read the manual. Cam knows her shit." West fell in love with a woman who runs the premiere business security company in the country, and she designed a custom system for me. This place is so far from civilization, there's no cell service, so the alarms won't contact any emergency services. But at least I'll know if anyone tries to break in. West had another member of the K&R team he works with—a hacker—zap all evidence this cabin even exists from every map on the internet.

"You want help moving shit inside?" West shoves his hands into the pockets of his leather jacket as Murphy pads through the front door and starts exploring our new home.

"Nah. Get out of here. I'll check in next week." The scent of fresh construction fills my nose as I inhale deeply. The inside is largely unfinished, which'll give me enough projects to get me through the summer. "Monday morning, 0900."

"Don't be late. Or I'll have a bird in the air in under an hour."

"I'm a goddamn SEAL, West. I don't need you *checking* on me once a month to make sure I'm still breathin'."

"I'm not checking on you. I'm checking on Murph." Dropping to one knee, West pats his other leg until my dog—a Belgian Malinois—trots over to him and sits. "Take care of this asshole. He's gonna need someone looking after him."

Murphy noses West's shoulder once, then dips his head so West can scratch him behind the ears. His tail thumps on the wood porch until I snap my fingers.

At the signal, he returns to my side immediately, though he knows there's no danger here. His tongue is lolling half out of his mouth.

"I mean it, Wyatt. You miss a check-in—even once—and I'll be up here so fast it'll make your head spin."

West clasps me on the shoulder, and I wince until he loosens his grip and mutters an apology. After almost losing my team in the ambush, I spent a solid month in the hospital and rehab before I could walk more than a few steps at a time or lift a cup of coffee with my right hand.

"Get back to Cam," I say through gritted teeth. Murphy presses his body to my legs, and I force myself to breathe through the pain that's more in my head than my limbs. "I won't disappear."

In truth, that's exactly what I want to do. Why I came up here. But West—and his team—pulled so many strings for me, they could weave a goddamn blanket if they wanted to. I purchased the land, but the construction, the security system, the solar panels...that was their doing.

All because seven years ago, I was part of the team that pulled Ryker McCabe out from under a snow-covered bush eight clicks from Hell Mountain. And ten days later, dragged

Kahlid—Hell's head torturer—from his hidey hole so Ryker and Dax Holloway, his brother in arms, could kill the man.

Once all my shit is put away—well after sunset—I crack open a beer and sink down onto the sofa. Murphy lies in front of the wood stove, basking in its warmth.

"This is ours, pal," I say quietly, toasting my best friend. He's the only reason I survived as long as I did in Seattle. Without him by my side, the panic attacks, the nightmares, the constant memories? They would have been too much. "No more sidewalks. No more people. No more constant *noise*. Just you and me and miles of nowhere to explore."

With a couple solid thumps of his tail, he lets me know he may not understand my words, but he's with me no matter what.

1

Hope

THE TUBE of concealer slips from my trembling fingers and the rosy tinted liquid splatters onto the pristine white marble countertop. "Shit." The bruises around my throat are *mostly* hidden, but now I have a mess to clean up.

A soft knock startles me as I run a washcloth under the faucet, and I yelp.

"It's me." Bettina—one of the housekeepers—slips through the bathroom door and shuts it behind her. "Mr. Simon left. He told Mr. Brix he would be back tomorrow."

I lean against the sink, relief making my muscles quiver and my eyes burn. Every time I swallow, I feel Simon's fingers digging into my neck, remember the look in his eyes as he squeezed hard enough I couldn't breathe.

"Miss Hope?" Bettina touches my arm. "Mr. Brix is in the gym for another thirty minutes. I can make sure no one goes near Mr. Simon's office. Now is your best chance." She reaches into the pocket of her uniform and pulls out a small memory card the size of my thumbnail. "This is what you needed, yes?"

I stare at the tiny piece of plastic in awe before I pluck it from her hand. "You found one."

"You were right. The grocery store had them. I snuck it in with the vegetables." The petite woman tucks a lock of black hair behind her ear. The swelling under her eye is better today, but she holds her left arm tight to her body. Simon twisted it so hard last week, I heard something snap. She can't go to the hospital—even if he *did* allow her to leave the house unsupervised. He keeps her passport locked in his safe, and her visa expired years ago. Long before she aged out of the biggest brothel in Salt Lake City and came to work at his compound. If her younger sister weren't one of his more *popular* girls, she'd already be dead.

"Come with me," I whisper. "He nearly broke your arm for talking to me. If he finds out you helped me escape, he'll kill you."

A single tear tumbles down her cheek. "I have no future, Miss Hope. I will never be...*free*. I have to stay close to my sister. She is all I have." Her eyes brim with tears, and she takes a step back. "Go now. I will do what I can."

I hug Bettina. A quick, fierce embrace. "If I live past tomorrow, it's because of you. I'll come back. When I have help. I'll get you out. I promise."

She offers me a small, wobbly smile, then wipes her eyes. "*Vaya con Dios*, Miss Hope. Do not worry for me."

As soon as Bettina leaves, I rush back into my bedroom, grab a small nail file, and drop to my knees in front of the heating vent. It takes me ten seconds to pry the metal cover from the wall—a move I've practiced dozens of times.

The only thing I still own in this world—a leather make-up pouch—holds close to five hundred dollars. Money stolen from Simon's wallet a few bills at a time over the past two years. My lifeline. In case I ever worked up the courage to leave.

If I'm lucky, it'll be enough to get me to Seattle. If not...I'll be dead. Assuming no one finds me in Simon's office first.

Tiptoeing down the stairs, I force myself to breathe when I round the corner. The house is quiet. Empty. Half a dozen guards patrol the perimeter of the compound—just inside the twelve-foot wall surrounding the whole place—but they never come inside unless Simon's here. Brix must still be in the gym. Closing myself in the office, I rest my back against the door. Thank God the laptop is still here.

"Everything you need is on this computer, Hope. It is not connected to the internet, so don't get any ideas. When you need information from the bank, you will ask me and I will get it for you. Understood?" Simon digs his fingers into my shoulders, squeezing hard enough to leave bruises.

"Y-yes. Please. You're hurting me."

He releases me and shoves my chair forward. "Get to work."

Every room in his house holds terrible memories, but I can't dwell on them now. I have to hurry.

Bettina's vacuum hums in the hall. She'll make a fuss if anyone comes.

Move, Hope. One foot in front of the other.

The desk feels like it's ten miles away, not ten feet. My hands shake, and I almost drop the memory card. Then insert it upside down. "Shit."

By the time I finish making copies of the files I need, my heartbeat roars in my ears loud enough to drown out the vacuum. Or maybe Bettina had to move further down the hall? How long has it been? A quick glance at the clock on the screen sends panic flooding through my limbs. Brix is almost done with his workout. I have to go. Right now.

Stripping out of my sweater, I tug at my bra. The tiny hole I made in the lining of the cup is just big enough to hide the small piece of plastic. If I can't get to the garage, if the Lexus keys aren't there, if anyone sees me...maybe I'll be able to keep the card a secret until I find another chance to run.

Another chance? Simon would never let you out of his sight again. If he even let you live.

By the time I crack open the office door, my inner voice catches up with reality.

He won't kill you. He can't. He needs you to hide his money. He'll just hurt you over and over again until you stop fighting. Until you're so broken, there won't be anything left.

The hallway is empty, the house utterly silent. No one will question the soft tapping of my boots on the travertine floors, but I'm so tense, each step sounds like a gunshot to my ears.

At the door to the courtyard, I stop and check all around me. Adrenaline tightens my chest, and sweat dampens my palms. *Go. Right now. Before anyone sees you.*

I'm going to make it. My fingers curl around the garage door handle, but before it opens more than a crack, a rough hand grabs my arm. I'm yanked back—so hard I stumble. My ass hits the ground. All the air leaves my lungs.

"Where do you think *you're* going?" Brix glares down at me, a snarl twisting his lips. "You're not allowed in there."

I can't talk. Can't breathe. Can't move. Until Bettina bursts through the French doors into the courtyard.

No.

"You leave Miss Hope alone!" she screams. Brix whirls. Just slow enough for Bettina to jump onto his back. Her good arm winds around his neck, and she holds on tight. Shit. *Move, Hope. Move!*

Breath rushes back into my body with a strained *whoosh.* Pushing to my feet, I lunge for the garage door. Seconds away, Brix pulls out a switchblade. It sinks into Bettina's forearm, and she crumples to the ground with a whimper.

"Run!" she cries. Lunging, she grabs Brix by the ankles. He

grunts, trying to shake her off. One punch. Two. Blood streams from her mouth. Still she holds on.

I'm frozen. Help Bettina? Or escape? I can't let her risk her life for nothing. She whimpers what might be the word "go."

I spin on my heel, but my indecision costs me. Pain slices through my left arm, hot and sharp. A heavy weight slams into my back. Down again, my knees crack against the flagstones. Another burning strike, this one to my thigh.

I kick with all my strength, and bone crunches under my boot. Brix roars. The weight lifts. Blood streams from his mangled nose. The knife is just out of his reach. I lunge for it, my fingers closing around the metal seconds before he realizes what I'm doing.

I can't fight him. He's too big. Too strong. Even with the blade, I'll lose.

Chucking it at his face, I turn and sprint for the garage.

"Bitch! Get back here!"

I slam and lock the door seconds before he reaches it. My gaze sweeps around the huge building. Simon collects cars like he collects brothels, and I have my choice of four different vehicles. The Lexus SUV is closest and, thank God, the keys are inside.

Brix's words are too muffled for me to hear as I start the car and jab the remote for the large rolling door, then the find the button for the gate in the perimeter wall. I made it this far. If I can make it out of town...if I'm fast enough...if I can get to the highway... Maybe I'll live long enough to make it to Seattle.

FIVE HOURS LATER, I pull into a gas station. Thank God I chose a dark red sweater this morning. No one can see the blood staining my sleeve. Or my black slacks.

I don't have a phone. Or a purse. Or any possessions. Just

the five hundred dollars in the center console. The attendant gives me a sideways glance when I slide four twenties across the counter. "Pump Six, please."

If I thought I had time, I'd load up on first aid supplies and treat the deep gashes to my bicep and thigh. But when I crossed into Idaho, I realized how stupid I was. The Lexus has GPS. Brix can track me. So I hand over another twenty for a couple of candy bars, a bottle of water, and a *Welcome to Idaho* t-shirt and try to hide my limp as I return to the pump.

I tear the t-shirt into strips while I fill the tank, then tie one around my arm and the other around my leg when I'm back on the road. Dangerous at seventy miles per hour, but so is bleeding to death.

Ahead of me, dark, ominous clouds fill the horizon. Eight more hours. Give or take. I should have bought a coffee. Or three. Flooring it up a hill, I pray I'm fast enough—or lucky enough—to still breathe free air tomorrow.

THE DAY IS LOSING its battle against the darkness, and the storm isn't helping. Flurries started an hour ago. Another thirty minutes, and I'll be over the pass. Or trapped in a blizzard.

My heart skips a beat—or three—when the passenger-side wheels leave the road.

I should slow down, but I have no idea how close Simon's men are. For ten hours, I've pushed the Lexus as fast as I dared, only stopping twice for gas. And to pee. Simon won't report the car stolen, but he'll track it—and me. Will he send Brix? And Matteo? And Tommy? Or call any one of the dozens of cops he has on his payroll?

It doesn't matter. Whoever he sends will make me wish I were dead.

I spare a glance at the dashboard. The temperature's dropped twenty degrees in the past hour. It might be spring on the calendar, but Washington State hasn't gotten the message yet.

My left arm throbs where Brix sunk his blade deep into my bicep. The strip of the gas station t-shirt helped stop the bleeding, but it still burns with every beat of my heart.

If only my thigh felt the same. It's mostly numb, and that can't be a good thing.

Lights flash in front of me, and I squint through the snow.

Hazardous Conditions Ahead.

Road Closed.

Exit Now.

"Shit."

No highway patrol cars, so I veer off the highway onto a mountain road. I hope the navigation system on the SUV is right about it rejoining I-90 in two miles. It's a huge risk and the road is bumpy as hell, but I don't have a choice. I'm still in the middle of nowhere, and if I stop, I die.

An hour of white-knuckling the steering wheel and I'm back on the interstate, but the weather's even worse now. Sleet hits the windshield in staccato bursts, making it difficult to see, and giant storm clouds rise to the heavens.

Accelerating out of a turn, I clench my jaw, my muscles screaming with how tightly I'm wound. How much longer until they find me?

Once I get to Seattle, I can dump the car and disappear. But until then...

Just keep driving. As fast as you can.

The back end of the SUV fishtails. "Shiiiiitt."

I manage to get the car under control seconds before bright lights flash behind me.

Oh, God. The road's closed. There shouldn't be anyone else out here.

I floor it, but the lights only get brighter. A *plink* hits the back window, and it turns into a spiderweb of cracked glass.

With a hole in it.

Oh, God. It's Brix. And he's shooting at me.

And then there's a loud pop. One of the rear tires wobbles. The SUV starts to spin.

Panic chokes me, and no matter how I turn the steering wheel, I can't get it under control. More sharp *plinks* to the side of the car. My left arm explodes in fresh agony. Blood splatters my cheek. Cold air whistles through a round hole in the driver's side window.

Before I can freak the fuck out about getting shot, the bottom drops out from under me, and I'm flying. Rolling. The world turns into a slow-motion video. Branches hit on all sides. White clumps of snow fly off the trees. The airbag deploys with a *whoosh*, hitting me square in the face.

I can't see. With my good arm, I bat at the deflating nylon. Still rolling. Sliding. It's so loud. Then almost...silent.

When the SUV stops, it's so sudden, my entire body jerks against the seatbelt. I'm...sideways. Lying against the door, the window above me shattered. The vehicle is rocking back and forth. Like some fucked-up teeter-totter.

The pain in my arm is almost overwhelming. Blood soaks into my sweater, so much it trails down my neck. Part of the windshield is caved in, and the airbag drapes over the steering wheel. Droplets of icy water pelt my cheek as the wind tears through the car.

I can't move. The seatbelt won't unlock. Everything hurts. I'm so dizzy, and the lights on the dashboard start to flicker. Where are Simon's men? Above me? Back on the highway? Can they see me down here? Do they know I'm still alive? If they do, I won't stay that way for long.

A wet tendril of hair falls over my eyes as I turn my head, and I struggle to brush it away. Even the smallest movements feel like I'm underwater, or wearing a shirt that weighs fifty pounds.

Stop the bleeding. Or you die.

But I can't. I can't move. Above me, a single beam of light sweeps back and forth. I think I hear voices, but they're so far away, I can't make out what they're saying.

Can they get to me? Even *see* me down here?

A shower of rocks hits the side of the car, and another window shatters. Those aren't rocks. They're bullets. I choke back a hoarse yelp, desperate to escape, but I can't.

I'm going to die. In the middle of nowhere, cold, and alone, and Simon is going to get away with killing me. Along with so many more...

2

Wyatt

MURPHY BOUNDS up to me as I finish stacking another load of wood against the cellar wall. His desperate barks raise the hair on my arms and tighten my chest in an all too familiar way.

Fuck. I haven't had a panic attack in months. Thought maybe I was over them—despite my former shrink warning me that wasn't very likely.

Dropping to one knee, I wrap my arms around my dog and touch my forehead to his. The Belgian Malinois—a type of Shepherd and my best friend in this world—stills until I can breathe again. He knows me. Knows what I need. Knows how to stop an attack from consuming me for hours.

With a low whine, Murphy licks my neck, and the cold swipe of his tongue helps pull me back from the edge. "I'm okay, pal. Good boy."

But he doesn't relax. Just lets loose with another series of barks as he bounds between me and the cellar door. "What is it?"

He skids to a halt, closes his teeth around my shirt sleeve, and tugs.

"Okay, okay. I'll follow you." After he leads me out of the cellar and I latch the doors, he runs to the edge of the meadow west of the cabin, then back to me. "Hold on. We're not going anywhere without our gear. Not today."

The sun set a bit ago, and the temps are falling fast. It only takes me a minute to snag my heaviest flannel from the peg just inside the cabin door and shrug into it with a wince. This weather's hell on my shoulder. But Murphy's vest—complete with a small emergency kit—is a little more complicated. He stands perfectly still as I tighten the straps, but his whole body is practically vibrating.

It's been months since he got excited about anything more than a family of rabbits searching for food, but whatever's got him all worked up today? It's serious.

"Hold up, Murph. Not taking any chances." I haven't seen another soul in almost two years—other than Old Man Parker at the General Store—but there are plenty of wild animals roaming this desolate area of the mountains, so I grab my field pack and sling my rifle over my shoulder before I lock the cabin door. It'd be just my luck we'd run smack into a bear.

Clouds, heavy and dark with snow, loom over the tall pines at the top of the cliff. A spring blizzard isn't unheard of, but this time of year in the Cascades is usually nothing but wildflowers and snowmelt. This storm, however, is rumored to carry more than three feet of accumulation.

The only reason I care? In under an hour, it's gonna start dumping, and I have no idea what Murphy's all worked up about.

"Show me," I say, giving Murphy permission to take off at a trot due west. Toward the storm.

Every five minutes or so, he stops and stares back at me. I'm not sure if he's scanning me for signs I'm too tired to go on or making sure I'm still following. Or both. We've been to hell and back together, and outside of one or two men in Seattle, he's the only other creature in this world I trust.

He yips and runs so far ahead, all I can do is follow his tracks. The snow starts falling, light flakes that hit my cheeks and melt instantly.

Shit. Where are you taking me, Murph?

Another mile and we'll reach the highway. People. Cars. Noise. No one ever stops, though. Nothing here worth stopping for. Not according to any published map or GPS. When you want to disappear, it helps to have friends with unlimited technical resources at their disposal.

I come around a bend to find Murphy scrambling over the rocks, winding back and forth as he climbs. We're halfway up the peak, and while this side of the mountain isn't too dangerous, the other side is nothing but sheer rock with a large crevasse sinking three hundred feet straight down.

Dusk along with the snow bathes the world in an eerie, gray glow. And then I see it. Lights cutting through the trees.

Murphy starts barking like he's just discovered the Holy Grail, and when I catch up to him, my jaw drops. A black SUV is pinned to the mountainside by a cedar tree. One that looks like it's about five minutes—or an inch of snow—away from snapping and sending the vehicle plummeting into the rocky maw.

"Shit. Murphy, back." As soon as I shout the order, the dog takes several bounding leaps behind me. "Hold."

He sits up tall, and I set my rifle down next to him.

"It's too dangerous for you, pal. Hold and wait."

From this angle, I can't see the driver. If they're even still in there. Digging in my pack, I pull out a flashlight. Is that...blood dripping from the window? I creep closer. Yep. Crimson stains the newly fallen snow. Fresh, so whoever's in there is still alive

—or was very recently—and they haven't been out here for long. Not in this cold.

Carefully, I pick and claw my way over the rocks until I'm above the SUV. The tree isn't going to last much longer. Not with the way the wind is picking up.

A woman lies against the driver side window. Pale skin, sunken eyes, and a fine layer of snow dusting her dark red sweater.

"Can you hear me? Uh...ma'am?"

I think her lashes flutter, but I can't be sure. "I'm gonna get you out of there. But whatever you do, *don't move*."

Shit. I don't even know if she *can* move. Or if she's still breathing.

Get your ass in gear, Wyatt. Or she's a goner.

Going in through the window above her is suicide. Any more weight on the tree trunk and it'll give up the ghost. But it's the only option. Even if it tips the SUV like a see-saw.

I pull a long length of rope from my pack and toss it over a broken tree stump just above the vehicle. It's a fresh break, probably from when the car fell, so the root system should be strong enough to hold me.

Without proper climbing equipment, this is going to be damn near impossible, but if I don't try, she'll die before I can get help. Either from hypothermia or when the tree snaps like a twig.

My gloves provide a good grip on the rope, and I lower myself hand-under-hand until my feet rest lightly on the door frame beneath her.

"Can you move, darlin'?" She doesn't stir, and there's way too much blood pooling on the cracked window for her to last much longer.

The seat belt's stuck. Shit. Letting go of the rope isn't an option. I'm a big guy. Six-foot-three, over two-fifty last time I got on a scale. So I wrap the rope around my left hand twice, and with my right, pull out my pocket knife.

I have to pry it open with my teeth, and sawing through the black nylon feels like it takes a century.

As soon as the belt gives way, the woman crumples forward with a tiny, weak cry. The SUV teeters. A loud crack reverberates through the air.

Her whimper turns into a hoarse scream. We're fucked. The tree won't last more than another few seconds.

"Focus, darlin'. I'm gonna get you out of here, but we have to hurry."

She blinks up at me, shock freezing her mouth in a small *O*. Crap. Another branch gives way. The SUV starts to tip forward.

"Can you tie this rope under your arms?" I ask, offering her the loose end. "As tight as possible."

She nods, but when she tries to shift, pain creases lines around her lips and her face turns white as a sheet.

"Stop. Never mind. We'll do it another way." This is a bad idea of epic proportions. "But we have to be fast. You understand?"

"Y-yes," she whispers.

"Is your right arm injured?"

"No." The woman gingerly reaches up, and I nod.

"Good. I need you to hang on to me. No matter what." Crouching a little lower, I slide my free arm around her back and lift her so she can cling to my neck. To her credit, she doesn't cry out, but she's shivering so violently, I'm afraid she's going to pass out any minute.

I guide the rope under her ass, then feed it through my belt loop. It's not enough to hold her entire weight. But it'll help. One more time around my body and I knot it at my shoulder.

Below us, Murphy starts barking, the tone frantic. "Gotta go, darlin'. Close your eyes if you have to, but don't let go."

She buries her face against my chest, and I pull us up one

hand at a time. She's maybe a buck-thirty, and I've carried heavier on missions. Granted, that was before the explosion.

Before the lifetime of pain and nightmares I just can't shake.

Six inches at a time, we rise. My head and shoulders clear the passenger side window as the tree gives up the fight. The crack is deafening, especially with the silence of the snowfall around us. The woman starts to scream.

"Look at me, darlin'. Nowhere else," I snap. She peers up at me, her brown eyes bloodshot and terrified, but she doesn't look away.

The SUV falls out from under us, and the crash when it lands? Fuck. I'm back in Afghanistan as the building explodes. I can smell the smoke. The burning flesh. The blood.

Until Murphy starts barking like his life depends on it. My best friend. He needs me. Cold fingers dig into the back of my neck. Blinking hard, I meet the woman's gaze. She's half frozen, and now that I can see her whole face? I'm back in the present in a heartbeat.

A black eye at least a week old. A scraped cheek, less than a day. Bruises around her neck. We're losing the light, but I wouldn't be surprised if those were finger marks.

Move, asshole. Get her onto solid ground.

"Almost there. This next bit's not gonna be fun." With the car gone, I brace my feet against the cliff face, bend my knees, and push off. We swing twenty feet to the right, and I absorb the worst of the impact as we come to rest before I lower us the last fifty feet.

Murphy runs back and forth, waiting for us, and as soon as we touch down, he presses himself to my legs. "It's okay, pal. Settle."

The command word calms him, and he sits patiently, waiting for my next order.

"What's your name?" I ask the woman in my arms. "I'll get

you up to the highway. There are call boxes every mile, and you need an ambulance."

She shakes her head, tears shimmering in her eyes. "No...hospitals," she whispers.

"You're bleeding, darlin'. And half frozen."

"He'll...kill...me." Her voice fades, her eyelids flutter closed, and she collapses against me.

"Fuck." What the hell am I supposed to do now?

3

Wyatt

I STUMBLE up the cabin steps with the woman slung over my shoulders in a fireman's carry. The whole trek, I was sure she was going to wake up and lose her shit, but I couldn't cradle her in my arms for two full miles. Not over rough terrain, in the dark, with the snow falling hard and fast.

Murphy sits patiently next to the wood stove while I lay the woman on the rug, stoke the fire that almost died out, and retrieve my first aid kit from under the kitchen sink. Now that I can see her in the light, I curse under my breath. I should have spent more time assessing her condition before hiking back here.

She's too pale. Her fingers are almost blue. I wrapped her in my heavy flannel before we set off, but she was already soaked to the skin and down a hell of a lot of blood.

"Can you hear me, darlin'? I have to get you warm, and that means taking these clothes off."

She's out like a light. If I thought I could wait until she regained consciousness, I would. The idea of stripping a woman down to her skivvies without permission doesn't sit well with me, but it's a hell of a lot better than watching her die.

Get your shit together, Wyatt.

Boots. I can handle taking off her boots. They're new. Expensive. As is her sweater. Hell, everything she's wearing screams luxury.

With every inch of skin I uncover, my anger ratchets up another dozen notches. Under the lights, it's painfully obvious she's been someone's punching bag for quite a while. Bruises cover her torso and upper arms, a handful of long, thin scars cross her back, and the wound to her left arm? It's not one gash, but two.

The deep slice was definitely from a blade, but just above the makeshift bandage she fashioned from a strip of cotton is a jagged hole. A bullet.

"He'll kill me."

Looks like whoever *he* is came damn close. I call up my memories of the SUV. One of the tires was flat. No glass in the passenger side window. The back window...at least three small holes.

Fuck me. Did they force her off the road too? I glance up at Murphy. "You heard the shots, didn't you, pal?"

He whines and nudges the woman's bare foot.

"I know. I'm workin' on it. No one's goin' to hurt her now." Not even me, if I can help it. But the bullet's still lodged in her arm, and I don't have any anesthetic. Now that her clothes—everything except her bra and panties—are in a heap next to the stove, her cheeks start to flush. Resting the back of my hand against her forehead, I mutter, "Shit." If she's this feverish after less than ten minutes inside...I need to get the slug out of her ASAP.

"Murph? Protect."

He knows hundreds of commands, and *protect* tells him to use his entire body to cover his target. Stretching over her, he rests his muzzle on her right shoulder. If she does wake up, at least she won't feel alone.

I have to dig into the wound with a pair of tweezers to find the bullet. Her weak cry upsets my best friend, but he does his job, nosing her neck until she calms. The hunk of metal falls into my palm. "Shit." It must have hit her *through* the seat, because a fragment of leather comes with it. No wonder she's burning up. The knife wound looks bad enough, the edges red and angry, and I need to get some antibiotics into her. Right fucking now. Or as soon as I sew her up.

"Just a couple of stitches, darlin'. Murph, stay put." I get to my feet with a groan, my hip and knee screaming at me to rest. Or down half a bottle of Vicodin—which isn't a path I'm willing to go down again. Been there, done that, ended up almost losing myself completely.

So I opt for a single shot of bourbon—all I ever allow myself—and sit back down to stitch her wounds. Either she's so far under she can't feel shit or Murphy's doing a damn good job of comforting her, because she doesn't stir.

Her thigh bears another knife wound, but this one doesn't need stitches. Just a solid cleaning and a sturdy bandage.

"I wish I had something else to call you besides 'darlin''. But it's gonna have to do until you wake up. Now, I'm sorry for this next part. But your bra's more blood than lace, and those panties didn't fare much better." I do my best not to look as I loosen the clasp, but maneuvering an unconscious woman into a t-shirt *without* seeing her breasts? Or...other parts? Almost impossible.

Laying her in my bed, I brush her dark brown hair away from her face. Her cheeks are bright red, and a cold compress isn't gonna do shit against a fever of 103. The antibiotic shot I gave her will help with the infection—*if* I can get her temperature down. I'd open the window if the storm weren't raging outside. Instead, all I can do is stick damp towels in the freezer and swap them out every fifteen minutes.

After an hour, she's worse, not better. Murphy whines from the foot of the bed. He's been restless ever since I brought her in here, and I think he's as worried as I am. "I know, pal. I'm trying."

"Darlin'?" I cup her cheek and pull back the blankets. "You're still burning up. I need to get that fever to break, and I only know one way to do that. Don't suppose you want to wake up for me, do you?"

No answer. I don't have much of a choice. A cold bath is the only option.

Stripping down to my briefs feels wrong, but she's barely stirred, and I don't trust my ability to keep her head above water unless I'm holding her.

Despite living "off the grid" up in the mountains, the large clawfoot tub is custom—long and wide enough for my bulk—and between the solar panels on the roof and my backup generator, hot water is easy to come by.

Wish I needed more of it now.

As soon as I sink down with her—and hiss out a sharp breath when my nuts try to crawl back inside my body—she whimpers and pushes weakly against my hold.

"Stay still," I snap. "You need this."

"Hurts." She collapses against my chest, her head lolling onto my shoulder. The single word is barely audible over the water pouring from the spout, but it's the first coherent one she's uttered since I got her out of the SUV.

"That's because you're burning up. Once that fever breaks, you'll feel better."

"Liar."

The fight in her tone reassures me, and I settle back, easing her a little lower in the water. "I was a United States Navy SEAL, darlin'. We *don't* lie."

"Isn't that what a liar would say?" she rasps.

"I suppose it is. But I'm not, and it's the God's honest truth. Don't suppose you have a name?"

"H-Hope..."

"That it? Just Hope?"

Her eyelids flutter, and she moves restlessly, her legs making tiny ripples in the water. The wet t-shirt clings to her hard nipples, and I squeeze my eyes shut.

Fuck. Stop thinking with your dick, asshole. She's barely conscious.

I might as well be talking to a wall for all the good it does me. Hope is gorgeous—even bruised, feverish, and bloodied—and there's something about her that calls to me. To the scarred, damaged, and broken pieces of my soul.

You're being ridiculous, Wyatt. She's in trouble, and as soon as the storm passes, you'll take her into town, call the sheriff, and never see her again.

Hope tries to turn towards me, but winces. A single tear rolls down her cheek.

"Easy now, darlin'. You're pretty banged up." With one arm tight around her waist, I use the other hand to check her forehead. "Your temp's better."

"Who...?"

"Wyatt. Wyatt Blake. I pulled you out of that SUV."

"Oh, God. Where are we?"

She's actually coherent now, though her voice doesn't rise much above a whisper.

"My cabin. About two miles from the highway. No roads up here in or out. You're safe."

Her right hand slips off the side of the tub and into the water. She tries to pick it up again, but her fingers curl around my thigh. "You're...naked?" Struggling to sit up and wriggle out of my arms, her breath stutters in her chest. "Let me go, asshole!"

"I'm not naked. Not an asshole either. At least not that kind of asshole. I'm wearing briefs. And you're in one of my t-shirts. Most everything you had on was bloody. I'll wash your clothes in the morning. And I'll let you go when you can sit up straight."

Hope pushes herself up, but after two seconds, swears softly and collapses against me. "Shit. I'm dizzy."

"You lost a lot of blood. And that slice to your arm is infected. Probably the bullet wound too. I gave you a shot of antibiotics, but you've been running a fever for hours." Reaching for the small infrared thermometer, I press it to her temple. "Let's see if we broke it." After the beep, I show her the screen. "Ninety-nine point six. Not bad. Time to put you to bed."

"B-bed?"

"You need to sleep. It's after 3:00 a.m. So you're going to let me help you into a dry t-shirt and carry you to my bed. I'll take the couch." When I pull her good arm around my neck and stand, her head lolls forward. "Well, shit," I mutter.

At least this way she won't see me mostly naked. It's not a pretty sight. Too many scars I don't want to explain.

She doesn't stir as I dry her off, get her into one of my well-worn Navy t-shirts, and tuck her under the covers. I pull on a pair of flannel pajama pants and a long-sleeved t-shirt to hide my scars, then ease a hip onto the bed next to her.

"Wyatt?" Bleary brown eyes struggle to focus on me, but at least she remembers my name.

"What do you need, Hope?" Brushing a lock of hair from her forehead, I try for a smile, but my entire body is one raw nerve. I need sleep as much as she does.

"What's...on my feet?"

My chuckle confuses her, and she pushes up on an elbow until I rest a hand on her shoulder. "Ease up. That's just Murphy. My dog. He's taken to you." I reach down to scratch

Murph behind the ears. "If you need anything, you tell him, 'Find Wyatt,' and he'll come get me."

She nods, her entire body relaxing against the pillows, and I think she's asleep before I stand up. "You keep watch, pal," I whisper to my four-legged companion. "All night."

Hope

Sounds filter in from somewhere close by. Footsteps, low murmurs, a deep voice talking to someone. Panic flares ice cold, and I sit up in this big, plush bed. Until my body reminds me I've been stabbed and shot and crashed my—well, Simon's—SUV into a tree halfway down a mountain.

I try not to make a sound, but obviously fail miserably, because a sleek, gray and brown dog bounds into the room and then barks once before jumping onto the bed and nosing my hand.

Those footsteps come closer, and it if weren't for the dog, I'd hide. Or try to. Not that there's anywhere to go.

"You all right, Hope?"

In the light of day, he's silhouetted in the door like some sort of angel, and my brain scrambles to remember his name, how I got here, and what he plans on doing with me.

"It's Wyatt, darlin'. And that's Murphy." Wyatt approaches slowly, his hands at his sides. "You were pretty out of it last night. Not surprised you don't remember much of me. But Murph might not be so understanding. He kept watch at your feet long past his breakfast this morning."

The dog slides his whole head under my hand, and he's so gentle and eager that I scratch behind his ears. Tail thumping on the bed, he lets his tongue loll out of his mouth and practically rolls over to show me his belly.

"Wyatt." I try his name, and bits and pieces of the night before come back to me. Terror. Cold. Pain. The SUV rocking back and forth like a seesaw on a tree. My voice is scratchy, and when I try to clear my throat, everything hurts. Back, arms, legs, *and* my head. "Shit."

"Don't try to move," Wyatt says. "I'll get you some water and Tylenol and then I need to check those bandages."

He's only a blur as he leaves the room, and I let Murphy wriggle closer. Whatever's going on—my brain's too fuzzy to put the pieces together—the dog, at least, feels safe.

"You always this...clingy?" I whisper as I let his silky ear slip through my fingers. He makes a happy sound and stares up at me like I'm his best friend. At least until Wyatt comes back in the room. Then his gaze locks on the big man and doesn't waver.

Even the most basic thoughts take more effort than they should, but the bond between these two is unmistakable. Murphy jumps down, rounds the bed, and settles himself on my right side while Wyatt takes a seat on my left.

"How much do you remember, Hope?" he asks, holding a thermometer to my temple. It beeps quickly, and he turns it towards me. "Ninety-nine-point-four. Still a little high for my liking. But it'll do."

"Not much." The words rasp over my raw throat, and Wyatt hands me two white pills. Squinting at them, I hope to God he's telling the truth and these really are just Tylenol.

"You want to see the bottle?"

I suck in a sharp breath. I shouldn't have pushed him. He'll be mad now.

"I wouldn't trust me either. Not after what you've obviously been through." There's no anger in his tone. Just...understanding. He takes a healthy swig from the water glass before passing it to me. "Nothin' but the cleanest mountain spring water you'll ever taste. I swear on my life. And Murphy's." The dog makes an inquisitive sound and lifts his head, and Wyatt chuckles. "If you don't trust me, maybe you'll trust him. I'll go get that bottle."

Everything about this man *screams* honor, and I shake my head. Slowly. Even that brings on a wave of dizziness, but it passes quickly. "S'okay. I'll take them. Anything to get rid of this drum solo behind my eyes."

He's right about the water. Or maybe I'm just that dehydrated. But when the glass is empty, he sets it on the nightstand and holds out his hand. "I need to check that arm."

Eyes closed, I let him unwrap the bandages. I'm not squeamish. Not usually. Hell, I managed to stop the bleeding *while driving* after Brix stabbed me. But while my mind isn't totally clear, I know if I look, every minute of the past two days will come rushing back to me, and I'm not ready for that yet.

"The bullet wound looks good. That other gash...I'm goin' to put on some fresh antibiotic and clean bandages. It'll probably hurt, and I'm sorry."

"Do it." Gritting my teeth, I prepare for the worst, but after the snap of a surgical glove, all I feel is a gentle pressure and a dull ache. One peek. I need to see how bad it is.

Two straight lines of stitches mar my upper arm, only inches apart. "You did that?"

"Yes, ma'am. Not my best work, but the scars should be minor. As long as you're careful." Wyatt doesn't meet my gaze, his whole focus on wrapping fresh gauze around my arm and binding it off with thick, white tape.

When he's done and all of his supplies are neatly arranged in the first aid kit, he sits back and runs his hands over his thighs. A pair of dark blue jeans mold to his legs, and he's wearing green flannel over a white t-shirt. "Are you hungry?"

Am I? I can't remember the last time I ate, but my stomach answers for me with a low, angry growl.

"I'll take that as a yes," Wyatt says, chuckling again. "Before

I cook, do you need to use the head? Given how much blood you lost, I'm not sure you should get up by yourself."

My cheeks flame as one particular memory from the previous night comes flooding back. Wyatt. Holding me. In the bathtub. Both of us mostly naked. "N-no. I'm fine."

He said he had to wash all of my clothes. Which means he saw... Oh, God.

My shame must be written all over my face, because he leans forward and nudges my chin up so I'm forced to look at him. "Hope? Whatever's going through your head? Let it go. You don't owe me an explanation. We're snowed in. Got more than five feet last night. There's nowhere you can go, but that also means no one's coming to find you. In a couple days, when the roads start to clear, you tell me what you want to do and I'll make it happen. Until then, you're safe with me."

Murphy rests his head on my thigh, as if he wants to reinforce everything Wyatt's saying.

Words are too hard over the lump in my throat, so I nod. Wyatt offers me a grim half-smile before striding from the room, and now I'm alone with this overly protective dog and no clue what to do next.

4

Wyatt

THANK fuck Hope finally opened her eyes. By 11:00 a.m., I was checking on her every ten minutes. If she'd slept much longer, I would have lost my shit.

More than once overnight, she cried out in her sleep, and after racing into the room for a third time to find Murphy pressed against her, nosing her neck or shoulder, I gave up, grabbed my blanket, and slept sitting up in the doorway only three feet from the bed.

The awkward position left my hip feeling like it's filled with broken glass, but being close to Hope was worth the pain. It calmed me. Settled me in a way I can't explain. And don't like. Not one bit.

In the kitchen, I pull out a pan and start the bacon. It's a damn good thing I hit up the general store a couple of days ago for a supply run. Otherwise, we'd be limited to smoked trout and...more smoked trout. Or MREs.

Scrambled eggs are about as fancy as I get, and I make up two plates, saving a couple of slices of bacon for Murphy. He earned a whole fucking steak for finding Hope last night, but after spending so many hours at her bedside, his dinner was nothing but kibble.

When I return to the bedroom, Hope's eyes are closed, but Murphy sits up at the scent of bacon, and she stirs at the movement. Her stomach rumbles, and she rolls onto her side with a quiet groan. "That smells...amazing."

"I can't cook worth shit. But eggs and bacon are hard to screw up."

She stares at the plate like it's mana from heaven. "I haven't had bacon in...almost three years."

Oh, fuck.

"You're a vegetarian? Shit. I have potatoes in the cellar. Canned green beans. I can try—"

"No. I love bacon." Wincing, she holds out her hands, and our fingers brush as I pass her the plate.

Her warm brown eyes water as she takes her first bite. After a little moan, she digs into the eggs. Watching her eat...it's like she hasn't enjoyed a simple breakfast in years. The food's gone in less than five minutes, and she hunches her shoulders and peers up at me like I'm going to be angry with her when I accept the plate from her trembling hand.

"Impressive. Want more?"

"I'm fine." With that flat tone to her voice, she's very *not* fine. And she's white knuckling the blanket like it's some sort of Kevlar vest.

"Hardly." My snort makes her flinch, but she needs to eat. Striding back into the kitchen, I retrieve my plate from the oven where I'd been keeping it warm and carry it back to the bedroom. "Hope? Are you still hungry?" Her gaze is glued to the six strips of bacon, and I arch my brows. "Answer me." As the words escape my lips, I realize my mistake, because her eyes fill with tears until she squeezes them shut. I should apologize. But I can't. My obstinance and her fear are locked in a standoff.

My inner voice orders me to back off, but I don't listen.

"Yes," she whispers.

"Then this is yours."

Murphy whines and sits up, like he *knows* if Hope asked, I'd probably give her the last two slices I saved for him too. "Outside. Do your business. Then food," I say.

He's out the door like a bolt of lightning, and I pass Hope the plate.

The second serving disappears just as quickly as the first, but she doesn't say a single word the whole time. Won't even look up at me until I take the plate from her. Then it's just a whispered, "Thank you."

"You won't go hungry here," I say, the words harsher than I intend before I return to the kitchen. Murphy pads back inside, sits, and raises one paw. "Good boy."

He stares up at me like I'm his whole world, and regret slams a sledgehammer against my chest.

She's injured. And afraid. She doesn't need you to be a complete asshole every time you talk to her.

The look on Murphy's face after I drop two slices of bacon into his bowl is nothing short of pure, canine joy, and I start the electric kettle. Clearing a path around the house this afternoon is going to take hours—and a couple of thermoses of instant coffee. Maybe if I bring Hope a cup, she'll forgive me. Or won't hate me quite so much.

Her color is almost normal when I return to the bedroom. Seeing her in my bed, looking like she belongs there, makes my dick twitch in my jeans. Another reason I need to spend the rest of the day outside.

Once I know she's taken care of.

"You want to try to get up? I haven't washed your clothes yet. Too cold to hang them in the cellar. But I got a robe that'll do well enough. The main room's warmer, and the couch is comfortable."

She blinks up at me, like she can't figure out why I care that she's warm. "Okay."

Back to one-word answers, almost devoid of personality, of emotion. If I weren't so sure she'd been abused—badly—for quite some time before ending up in my bed, I'd be tempted to take her by the shoulders and shake her. Anything to get a rise out of her. Or see a fraction of the enthusiasm she showed for breakfast. But like a wounded animal, she needs tending. Care. Gentleness. All things I'm shit at.

Snagging my robe from the back of the door, I hold it out to her, but she shies away from me.

Assess. Adapt. She won't believe it if you tell her she's safe. Show her.

I drop the robe next to her and back away. "I won't touch you unless you ask me to, Hope. And I sure as shit won't hurt you." With my hands shoved into my pockets, I wait for her to pull the thick, flannel-lined cotton to her chest.

"I don't know you," she whispers. Her eyes give her away. She *wants* to trust me. She just can't.

"You probably don't remember much from last night, but I spent more than a decade as a Navy SEAL. Retired a little under four years ago. Moved up to the mountains six months later."

"And that's supposed to make me feel better?" Hope tries to shove her left arm into the sleeve, but the pain must be too much for her, because she drops the robe and barely manages to stifle her whimper.

"Well, yeah," I say, keeping my voice as gentle as possible. "We have a code."

Now it's her turn to snort. Or huff. The sound tugs at the corners of my lips. Until she meets my gaze. "Just because you're a soldier doesn't mean you're a good guy."

Bristling, I run my hand over the short beard I let grow out once I moved up here. "First of all, the only *soldiers* in the United States armed forces are in the Army. I'm a SEAL. Second, if I'd wanted to hurt you, I could have done it any time in the past eighteen hours. Or left you in that SUV rather than risking my life to get you out. And third? Do I *look* like I'm a monster?"

"Most monsters look perfectly normal."

The words are so quiet, if I hadn't been holding my breath, I wouldn't have heard them.

"I've never hit a woman, and I'm sure as fuck not going to start now." After a heavy sigh, I hold out my hand. "Will you let me help you? Please?"

Hope tries one more time to lift her arm, then nods and pins her gaze to the edge of the mattress. Gently, I wrap my fingers around her wrist. Her skin is soft, and still a little too warm, but the antibiotics are helping. Another day and she'll be out of danger. At least from the infection.

"Keep your arm as still as you can. Just like this. I'll slide the sleeve onto your shoulder." She doesn't move—I'm not even sure she breathes—as I tug the robe around her and secure the belt. "Get up slow. You lost—"

"A lot of blood. I know," she says, twin notes of fear and anger in her tone.

Holding up my hands, I retreat far enough some of the tension leaves her body, but not so far I can't catch her when her legs wobble and she pitches forward.

"Shit. I didn't think it'd still be this bad..."

"The dizziness?" She feels like heaven in my arms. Too thin. Too weak. But I can see the woman underneath the bruises and a whole heap of PTSD. *That* Hope stares up at me like I hold the answers to life itself. Until she blinks, and all that emotion shutters so fast, I can almost *hear* it. "You need more food. And rest. Murphy will take care of you today."

I scoop her up and carry her out into the main room. A fire roars in the wood stove, and she stares out the big picture window. The porch running all around the cabin provides a buffer from the storm, but beyond the weathered wood, tall drifts obscure everything but the tops of the trees.

Her breath quickens, and her body, which *was* soft and loose in my arms, tenses. "Oh, God. We really are...trapped here."

"Trapped is a harsh way of putting it," I say, easing her onto the sofa and draping a blanket over her legs. "I have a snowmobile in the shed. I can get us to the General Store a few miles away if I have to. But it'd be slow as fuck and twice as dangerous. At least for the next day or two. You have somewhere you need to be?"

I'll settle for anything from her at this point. Any small bit of information she's willing to share.

But she shakes her head and shrinks before my eyes, burrowing into the robe and under the blanket like they can protect her from everything bad in this world.

"Hope?" I brush a wavy lock of hair away from her forehead. "One good thing about all that snow? We might not be able to get out, but no one's getting in either. Try to relax. Rest. I need to take care of a few things outside—clear off the solar panels, move a few stacks of wood onto the porch to dry. But I'll be close. You need anything, you tell Murphy."

She nods but doesn't meet my gaze, staring into the flickering flames like I'm not even here. I'm shit at small talk unless I'm on mission, and even then...I mostly left that up to the rest of the team. If she wants her secrets, she can have them.

For now.

Hope

I'm not sure how long I doze on the couch in front of the fire. Or what time it was when I first woke up this morning. I haven't seen a clock since I got here. Or a phone.

Wyatt comes in and out a handful of times to refill his thermos, check my temperature, and offer me jerky, water, and instant coffee—the only type he has, apparently. I'm not used to being fussed over. Though his version of fussing mostly involves grunting short, terse sentences. "Are you comfortable? Do you need anything? You should eat more."

Murphy lies at my feet the whole day, but he doesn't sleep. If I didn't know better, I'd think Wyatt ordered him to keep watch over me. I haven't spent much time around dogs, but intelligence shines in his big brown eyes, and having him close by makes me feel like I'm not so alone in the middle of nowhere.

An eerie silence holds sway over the cabin, broken only by the sounds of Wyatt working outside. Rhythmic chopping, the scrape of the shovel, and the occasional heavy footsteps criss-crossing the roof. More than once, the sudden noise causes me to jerk awake.

Darkness covers the windows by the time I feel strong enough to make it more than the few steps from the couch to Wyatt's bookcase. His collection of reading material baffles me. Biographies, history books, a handful of volumes in languages I don't recognize, science fiction, fantasy, thrillers—even a couple of romance novels.

As much as I'd like to just sit and read a book for pleasure—something I haven't done in three years—I have to find my bra. And the memory card hidden in the lining of the cup.

Murphy stays close as I shuffle into the bedroom, check around the bed and in the bathroom, but find nothing.

"Any ideas?" I ask him. He cocks his head and his ears perk

up, but all he does is grab the sleeve of the robe gently between his teeth and try to tug me out of the bedroom. "You're probably hungry, aren't you? I'll see if I can find you something to eat."

We don't make it to the kitchen, though. Because before we reach the couch, the front door opens, and Wyatt stomps inside. The image of him in full flannel, a fleece-lined hat on his head—red and black plaid no less—with a rifle slung over his shoulder is equal parts sexy, hilarious, and terrifying.

"Feelin' better?"

"Where are my clothes?" I demand, forcing my voice to remain steady, despite how scared I am.

"In the cellar." He peels off his hat and hangs it on a hook by the door, then sets the rifle in the corner. "Clearing the solar panels took a hell of a lot longer than I'd planned. I'll get to 'em after dinner."

"I need my bra." At his raised brows, I add, "Please."

"My t-shirt not doin' it for you? It's the best one I own."

I touch the collar of the soft cotton emblazoned with the Navy insignia. "It's not that..." I can't risk telling him the truth. He put a target on his back pulling me out of that SUV. If he finds out who I really am—and who hurt me—he'll be in even more danger. The less he knows, the better. My legs start to shake, and Murphy nudges me back toward the couch. The dog's right. Being upright for ten minutes has left me feeling like death, and I was so warm and comfortable all day. But I need that bra. So instead, I trudge in the direction Wyatt indicated.

"Goddammit, Hope. I'll get you the bra. But you're going to sit down before you fall down and I toss the fucking thing out the back door."

His growl is both possessive and frustrated, and it makes the fine hairs on my arms stand up. I should be frightened. But when Wyatt gets all gruff and protective, it's comforting. Like there's nothing he won't do to keep me safe. He stomps away, and a moment later, a door at the back of the kitchen opens and shuts.

Murphy bites down on the robe's sleeve and tugs gently.

"Okay, I'm going. Geez. You and Wyatt are two of a kind." Sinking down, I blow out a breath. Everything hurts, but when the dog jumps up next to me and rests his head on my thighs, I drape my good arm around him and let his warmth seep into me.

It doesn't take Wyatt more than two minutes to return with my bra dangling from his fingers.

"It won't bite, you know," I say at the look in his eyes. My lips start to curve into a smile until I see the blood staining the left cup. My blood. And not a small amount of it.

"Hope?" Wyatt crouches in front of me with a grunt. "What's wrong?"

"N-nothing. I didn't realize..."

Understanding dawns, bringing a scowl to his face. "That you almost died? Yeah. The plates on the SUV were from Utah. Just how long were you driving with that gash in your arm? Eight? Ten hours?"

I nod, panic setting in. He knows where I came from. Or has an idea, anyway. How long until he figures out exactly how much trouble I'm in?

"You really want to wear this again? I can wash it right now, but I do all my laundry by hand. There's no washer or dryer here. Best I can do is hang it over the wood stove. I'll do it. Just say the word. But you'll have to stare at it for the rest of the night."

I snatch the blood-stained lace from his hand. "I'll take care of it myself."

"Goddammit, Hope. You're in no shape to stand at the sink for half an hour getting blood out of anything right now." Wyatt tries to take the bra back, but I clutch it to my chest. Rolling his eyes, he pushes up, winces, and shakes his head. "Fine. I need half an hour to soak in the tub. Moving all that snow and wood did me in. Then I'll make us some dinner. If it warms up by morning, I might be able to get you to the General Store—and a phone—tomorrow afternoon. Until then, you can ignore me for all I care."

He limps off to the bedroom, and the door slams with a finality that has me ready to run. And makes Murphy lift his head with an inquisitive sound.

"Is he always this...ornery?" I ask. I don't know why I expect an answer. Even if the dog *could* give me one, he'd be loyal to Wyatt.

Alone—except for those luminous brown eyes watching me with interest—I dig my fingers into the layers of lace. Thank God. The memory card's still there. Even more of a miracle? It's not covered in dried blood.

I risked my life leaving Simon. I probably got Bettina killed. Tears burn my eyes, and I wrap my arm around Murphy and let myself break. Helping me? Attacking Brix? There's no way Simon would have let that go. She was the only person I could talk to. The only one who ever risked talking to *me*. And she's dead because of me. I can't let the same thing happen to Wyatt.

This card is the only way I'll ever be free, and even *it* might not save me in the end. But I have to try.

Wyatt

Hot water rushes into the tub, and steam obscures my reflection in the mirror. I should take the damn thing down. It's not like I *want* to be reminded what my scarred body looks like. But in the summer, I get the itch to shave, and using a straight edge without being able to see what I'm doing? That's a recipe for disaster. Or a few more scars.

Up here, though...who'd care? Old Man Parker at the General Store? He'd just shake his head and add one more check mark to the "Wyatt's a reclusive whack job" list I know he keeps behind the counter somewhere.

Sinking down into the water, I stifle a groan. My hip started locking up three hours ago, and my right shoulder hasn't fared much better. Shoveling snow is hard, back-breaking work, and I stayed out twice as long as I'd planned. All to make damn sure the generator was clear and none of the connections on the solar panels had come loose.

And maybe so I wouldn't have to remember what *polite conversation* feels like.

But now, I'm stuck. It's dark, close to freezing outside, and the snow is too thick to get to what barely passes for a town in these parts. Maybe if I feed Hope enough, she'll be so tired, I can put her to bed and pretend my solitary life is still just as solitary.

Who do you think you're kidding?

All fucking day, every time I stopped moving for more than a minute, I'd see those bruises around her throat. The ones on her upper arms. The scars across her back.

Or I'd hear her voice.

"He'll kill me."

No one's going to hurt her while I'm around. But what happens when I let her go?

"I humbly serve as a guardian to my fellow Americans. Always ready to defend those who are unable to defend themselves."

The day I earned my Trident, I was on top of the world. Of course, I was also fucking exhausted after celebrating the entire previous night with the other men who stood with me. Brothers. All of them. Most are dead now. West Sampson. Ace Marklin. Finn Hernandez. They're the only ones left.

I'll never serve again. My Trident is locked in my safe, and that's where it's going to stay. But once a SEAL, always a SEAL. And that means I'll protect Hope for as long as she'll let me.

Running my hand down my torso, I grimace as my fingers trace the raised shrapnel scars dotting my abs. They blaze a trail lower, stopping a half inch from my dick. The docs warned I might never be able to have kids. Hell, I'm lucky I can still get it up. The explosion left me with nightmares, nerve damage, and a permanent limp. Reminders to *always* trust my gut.

Now, it's telling me that Hope is in serious trouble. The kind that doesn't stop at running a woman off the road. Whoever's after her might be slowed down by all this snow, but in a couple of days, nothing's going to stop them from canvasing every inch of this mountain looking for her.

When my muscles stop screaming at me, I pull on a long-sleeved Henley, a pair of flannel pajama pants, and thick socks. This is going to be a long night. I should have washed Hope's clothes first thing this morning, but I couldn't drag myself down the stairs—and away from her—long enough to run the water. To be fair, I'm not sure any amount of detergent will get that blood out.

Digging through my drawers, I find a second pair of flannel pants. They're at least six inches too long for her, but a pair of scissors will fix that. The tie at the waist should cinch tight enough to hold them up. Maybe she'll feel more like herself with something besides a robe to protect her.

At the door, I stop, finally able to put a name to this churning sensation in my gut. Nerves. Uncertainty. *Fear.*

I've jumped out of planes more times than I can count. Spent six years in a war zone where any day could have been my last. And the prospect of spending time with Hope terrifies me.

Time to nut up, asshole. She's a woman. Not a witch. And she needs you.

5

Hope

ALL ALONE, I sob against Murphy's neck. When I ran, everything happened so fast. Copying the evidence I needed, fighting Brix, watching Bettina try to help me. Then, my entire focus was on making it to Seattle.

Now, the weight of what I've done—of Bettina's death, of the danger I'm putting Wyatt in—feels like it's crushing me. Simon hurt me whenever he felt like it. Whenever I *disobeyed* even a little. But he only hurt *me*.

I should have stayed. No matter how bad it got. Or...

Murphy wriggles closer—as if he can sense my thoughts. More than once over the past three years, I prayed Simon would kill me. That he'd get so angry, he'd go too far. Hurt me too badly for anyone to fix. I used to think that would be for the best.

I cry silently—another skill I mastered in the past three years—until I don't have any tears left. Swiping at my cheeks with the sleeve of Wyatt's robe, I sniffle once and meet the dog's inquisitive gaze.

"Probably should have asked Wyatt for a handkerchief, huh? He doesn't strike me as the kind of man who uses tissues." I don't know why I'm talking to Murphy like he can understand me. Except, there's so much intelligence behind those eyes. And he isn't judging me. Not even for blubbering all over him.

The bra fell to the floor sometime during my crying jag, and when I bend to retrieve it, the room spins a little. "Crap. Guess it's staying there." Murphy jumps off the couch, sniffs the blood-stained lace, and whines. Even he's not touching it. Can't say I blame him.

The bedroom door's still closed, but the water in the tub stopped running a few minutes ago. Before Wyatt comes back, I have to find somewhere to hide the memory card. And since I can't put the bra back on—even if I *could* twist my left arm behind my back to do up the clasp—I need another option.

What I wouldn't give for pockets. My *own* pockets. Or my little makeup bag. Shit. The cash. It was in the center console of the SUV. Now it's probably buried under five feet of snow.

That's the least of your problems, Hope. Hide the memory card. Then you can figure out how you're getting to Seattle.

Universal truth. Everyone has a junk drawer. Even a tall, grumpy mountain man who wouldn't know polite conversation if it bit him on the ass. And everyone's junk drawer has to have a roll of tape in it.

The dog stays close as I shuffle into the kitchen. I don't know if he's more worried I'm going to fall over or steal something. "Stay quiet, okay?" I whisper. He sits and watches me open drawer after drawer. Silverware. Cooking utensils. Knives. All precisely organized. Shit. Was I wrong? Maybe he *doesn't* have a junk drawer.

Nothing in Wyatt's cabin is out of place. The books on the shelf are in alphabetical order by author. I haven't seen a single knickknack. Nothing personal. The wood plank walls are bare.

I think I saw a photograph on his dresser, but that's the only indication he does anything but exist here.

Opening the last drawer, I blow out a shaky breath. Still neat and tidy, but it's definitely a mishmash of...well, everything. Tape, scissors, paperclips, safety pins, a small sewing kit, a notepad, and one very expensive fountain pen.

I tear off a three-inch strip of tape and secure the card under my left breast. Not the best place. The small of my back would be better, but there's no way I can reach it without taking off the robe. And if I did that, I might not be able to get it back on again. Not with how useless my arm is.

With slow, careful steps—the short foray from the couch used up all the energy I have—I return to the living room. The tape isn't comfortable, but keeping the card on my body is the safest option. Even if Wyatt has to change the bandages on my arm, he won't be able to see under the shirt.

As soon as I pull the blanket over my legs again, Murphy curls up next to me like we never moved at all.

I stroke the soft fur behind his ears, and his tail thumps gently. "You like living out here in the middle of nowhere? Lots of squirrels and birds to chase?"

"He loves squirrels. Hates the crows who try to dive bomb him every spring." Wyatt's deep voice shocks me, and I yelp, sending Murphy to full alert. He presses his body to me like a shield, then noses my neck with a whine.

"Oh, God. Are you always that quiet?" My bruises protest when I twist around, and I hiss out a breath.

Wyatt shrugs, and his cheeks take on a hint of color. "Part of the training. I don't even think about it. Murph, settle." The dog relaxes instantly, and Wyatt skirts the couch to stand in front of me.

I have to crane my neck to meet his gaze, and his stare is so intense, I quickly avert my eyes. Panic starts to tighten a band around my chest. Shit.

Don't let him see how scared you are. He hasn't hurt you yet. Maybe...he won't. Maybe he's just a good guy. A good, scary guy. Just...breathe.

He crouches down so we're on the same level, and his expression softens. "Look at me." All I risk is a quick glance. I can't read him, but a hint of warmth tinges his voice. "Thought you might be more comfortable with some pants," he says, offering me a bundle of faded gray flannel. "I can cut the legs shorter for you."

The gesture is sweet—and unexpected—but I won't take anything else from this man. Except food. And shelter for one more night. We are snowed in after all. I already owe him more than I can repay.

"You don't have to mutilate your clothes for me."

"Hope..." There's that tone again. The one that says he won't take no for an answer. Every time Simon used that tone, I knew I was in for a beating. But with Wyatt...I think hurting me would kill him. "Put them on. Please? I'll get the scissors."

I *would* feel better if I weren't half naked. More confident. Less like a wounded bird afraid to be stepped on. And he said please.

"Fine." Slipping my feet into the pant legs, I maneuver the pajamas halfway up my thighs, then push up to standing. There's a tie sewn into the waistband, but I'm so wobbly—and a little dizzy—I fumble with the strings. Nope. Can't do it. Not with the robe in the way.

Even with the belt undone, it's a challenge. My hands tremble, and fresh tears burn my eyes. This isn't rocket science. Or a marathon. I should be able to manage one simple bow. But I can't.

"Let me." Wyatt's fingers are warm, calloused, and gentle as he secures the tie, then lowers himself to one knee in front of me. From the lines tightening around his lips, the motion causes him pain, and I want to ask him what's wrong.

Before I can find the words, I'm distracted by how the black Henley clings to his shoulders. By the scent of his soap—*Irish Spring* if I had to guess—and the way his hair curls ever so slightly over his collar.

"There." Rising with two scraps of flannel in his hands, he arches his brows. "Better?"

"Yes." It doesn't matter that everything's too big on me. That the thick socks are twice as long as I need, that the t-shirt hits me mid-thigh. Every part of me is covered and warm, and no one's hurt me since Wyatt pulled me out of the SUV.

As he turns to the kitchen, I grab his arm. "Thank you."

"They're just pants. Old ones." He shrugs, preparing to shake off my hold, but I tighten my fingers on his wrist.

"I mean for everything. Taking care of me. Making me breakfast. Not...prying." I take a step closer, but my legs aren't steady. I pitch forward, right into Wyatt's chest. His very warm, very hard chest. His arm bands around my waist, and we're so close, I can feel the beat of his heart.

"Whoa. You're not ready to be upright yet, darlin'. At least not for long."

Oh, God. I didn't know how much I needed someone—needed *him*—to hold me like this. It's been so long since anyone's touched me with kindness. Offered comfort. Safety. Right now, I have all of that and more wrapped up in this gruff, handsome package.

"Wyatt." I breathe his name, and his groan tells me he's as affected by this as I am. "Please."

"Please what...?"

Sliding my uninjured arm around his neck, I pull myself up onto my toes and touch my lips to his. For a brief second, we're one. Connected in a way I've never felt before. I think Wyatt senses it too, because when I break off the kiss, the look in his eyes? Desperation. Pure, raw need. And longing. But then he blinks, and all that emotion vanishes.

"This is a bad idea." He deposits me back on the couch and, before I can say another word, strides for the kitchen.

Great. Just how much more grumpy, alpha male can I handle?

Wyatt

I can't read Hope. One minute, she's defiant and almost snarky. The next, timid and afraid. And just now? That kiss took guts.

As soon as I'm out of her line of sight, I touch my fingers to my lips. I'm no saint. I've had my share of one-night stands. Even paid for an escort or two when I was young and stupid and deployed overseas. Serious relationships aren't my thing.

But with her? I'm starting to want something more. Something I can't have. Leaning against the counter, I will my dick to calm the fuck down. Hope has only been here for twenty-four hours, and while I've managed to chain my demons so far, how long until they break free and Hope sees who I truly am?

If there's a God, she'll be gone before that happens.

And you'll be alone. Again.

For the first time in three years, the idea of a solitary existence with only Murphy for a companion fills me with something other than relief.

Get out of your own head. Hope needs food, and so do you.

"Steak and potatoes okay?" I ask as I pull out the cast iron pan, then peer back around the corner. "Don't have a lot of variety this time of year. Unless you want bacon and eggs again."

"I can eat anything." Frowning, she wrinkles her nose. "Except tofu. I don't ever want to see another piece of tofu again. In any form."

After I set a pot of water to boil, I start seasoning the steaks and scrubbing the potatoes. "No tofu here. I think Old Man Parker would laugh me out of his store if I asked him to order me some of that shit."

Hope pushes to her feet and makes her way into the kitchen.

"Thought I told you to say put?"

The look she shoots me is nothing short of indignation. "You didn't tell me to *do* anything. Just said, 'this is a bad idea,' and walked away."

Well, shit. "You need to rest."

"I need to feel like a human being." Cradling her left arm with her right, she leans against one of the exposed wooden beams at the entrance to the kitchen. "Why do you live all the way out here?"

"Better for everyone." At her huff, I turn my attention to the stove, hoping that'll put an end to this line of questioning, but she doesn't back down and clears her throat. Defiant Hope is back. I flick my gaze to hers, finding her watching me closely. "Too much noise in the city."

"Noise. And that made you come all the way out here? You couldn't have split the difference and moved to the suburbs? You're in the middle of nowhere."

"If I weren't, you'd be at the bottom of the ravine." It's the wrong thing to say by a thousand miles, and Hope's shoulders hike up to her ears. "Fuck. I'm sorry. This is why I'm better out here. I don't *do* small talk. Or niceties. I'm an asshole. One hundred percent. And you should go back to the couch."

Way to lean in.

I don't expect her to straighten. Or take two steps closer as I add the salt and potatoes to the boiling water. "You're a smart guy, Wyatt. Your bookshelf is full of nonfiction and classics—along with the oddest collection of science fiction, thriller, and fantasy novels I've ever seen—and they're not for show. All the spines are broken. You can't tell me you don't know how to make conversation. And I don't believe for a hot minute that you're anywhere near as much of an asshole as you think you are."

"I know *how* to talk to people." My voice takes on a hint of exasperation, and some of my demons start clamoring to be released. "SEALs don't just know how to fight. We're trained to blend in. We need to be able to operate on foreign soil without raising any eyebrows. We spend as much time in the classroom as we do in the water. So yeah. I'm smart. Smart enough to know I'm too fucked in the head to be around people on the regular. *That's* why I live way out here. Because if I didn't, I'd go off on my neighbors for slamming their door one too many times or shooting off fireworks on the Fourth of July. Or worse. I'd spend half my nights huddled in a closet because it's the only place I'm certain no one's going to sneak up behind me."

My outburst has her stepping back, horror and sadness welling in her eyes.

"Go sit down," I snap. "It'll be another fifteen minutes until the food's ready, and I'm not going to spend the whole of it explaining myself to you."

Watching her slink away is harder than all the work I did today. Harder than anything I've done in months. Maybe years. And when she eases herself back down onto the couch and wraps her good arm around Murphy, tears glisten on her cheeks.

But it's her whispered, "I'm sorry," that has me wanting to punch a hole in the wall—even though it's solid wood. It was barely loud enough for me to hear, and the way her back shakes as she clings to my dog is enough to destroy me.

I can't be...human. Can't be around people. No matter how much I want to change, I'll never be anything more than a broken recluse who's better off alone.

6

Hope

MURPHY DOESN'T LEAVE my side until I stop crying. As soon as I let go and sit up straighter, he pads into the kitchen to join Wyatt. Alone—despite the six-foot-four self-proclaimed asshole cooking me dinner twenty feet away—I stare at the flames flickering in the stove until my eyes unfocus.

Why didn't I listen? Just mind my own business and let him have his secrets?

Because you needed someone to talk to. Because he saved your life. Because you're wearing his pants. His shirt. His robe.

With every reason I tick off, I feel worse. The past three years have been one bad decision after another, and now I'm snowed in with a man who hates me.

No more crying. Certainly not in front of Wyatt. He may *think* he has some social skills, but he's wrong. Or he just doesn't care to use them. I'm not sure which is worse.

I'm so tired of feeling uncomfortable in my own skin. Of second guessing everything. Of being afraid. I used to think I was strong. Independent. Able to take care of myself. Until Simon.

Now the idea makes me laugh. I didn't stand a chance against a master manipulator with a plan. Simon turned breaking a person down into an art form, and by the time I realized what he was doing, I was trapped. No way out. Cut off from the world. My friends. My whole life.

The sizzle of the steak in the pan helps distract me. As does the scent. My stomach growls and twists in on itself. I'd offer to help if I thought I could stand for more than a few minutes at a time.

Who am I kidding? That would involve talking to Wyatt again. Not going there until I have to.

Peering out the window, I'm shocked at how utterly dark it is outside. No street lights. No city glow. The glass is pitch black. I can't even see the snow. Are Simon's men looking for me? Or do they think I died in the crash? I reach down and feel for the memory card taped to my skin. Simon owns the police in Salt Lake City. The FBI agents too. Seattle was the closest big city that felt *safe*. But what if I was wrong? What if I get there—somehow—and he finds me anyway?

"Dinner," Wyatt announces, breaking through the thoughts racing around in my head. "What do you want with it? Only three choices, really. Water, coffee, and bourbon."

"I haven't had a drink in three years. Bourbon would probably knock me right out." The number of things I've missed could fill a football field, and I brace my hand on the back of the couch as the weight of it all slams into me. "Water's fine."

After a beat, Wyatt frowns, but fills two glasses from the tap and sets them on a small dining table in the corner of the main room. Food has never smelled so good. Not since breakfast, anyway.

I suppose when you spend three years eating all the foods you *hate*—tofu, vegetables with every ounce of flavor boiled out of them, and wheatgrass—anything might smell and taste amazing.

Wyatt reaches for my arm when a wave of dizziness hits me steps from the table, but I wave him off and lean against the wall until it passes. "I'm fine."

"The hell you are." He checks my forehead, and some of the worry lines etched around his lips ease. "Your fever hasn't come back, but fuck, Hope. You almost bled out twenty-four hours ago. Let me help you."

"You've made it very clear you'd rather not talk or interact beyond the minimum. I'm trying to respect that." Despite my words, I let him help me to the hard wooden chair. "I just need rest. And food. I'll be fine in the morning."

He snorts, but doesn't argue, and when he sets a plate twice the size of my head in front of me, my mouth waters.

"I didn't ask. Is medium rare okay? I can let it cook another few minutes..."

"And ruin what looks to be a perfect cut of meat? Don't you dare." The first bite is so good, I moan, and the corners of Wyatt's mouth twitch. I used to dream of meals like this. The first few months, all I wanted was a hamburger. French fries. After a year, I would have killed for a piece of toast with butter. Carbs. Sugar. Caffeine.

We eat in silence for several minutes until Wyatt clears his throat. "Hope? Don't ever apologize to me like you did earlier. *I* was the asshole. You didn't do anything wrong."

Instinctively, my shoulders curve inward, and I hold my breath. In my world, men don't admit they screwed up without an ulterior motive, and whenever Simon apologized, it was usually followed by, "But I have to punish you now."

"Hope?" Wyatt asks, reaching across the table to skim his rough fingers over the back of my hand. "You were fine, and now you're not. Who is he and what did he do to you? Because once this snow clears, I'm gonna hunt him down and beat the ever-loving fuck out of him."

"No! You can't!" My fork clatters to the plate, bounces, and ends up on the floor, where Murphy pounces on it like it's prey.

"Dammit, Murph. You'll get your own bowl when we're done. Sit and hold."

The dog immediately returns to his place by Wyatt's chair, drops down to his haunches, and does his best impression of a statue.

After he passes me a clean fork, Wyatt rests his hands on his thighs and pins me with an unwavering stare.

"I'm a grown-ass man, Hope. Pretty sure I'm still able to throw a punch. Give me one good reason why I shouldn't teach that asshole a goddamn lesson."

"Because he'll kill me. And you." The idea of putting Wyatt in danger—any more than I already have—leaves my stomach in knots, and I push the plate away.

He slides it back in front of me, the defiance in his eyes sending my gaze to my hands clasped in my lap. "I'm damn hard to kill, darlin'."

"Not for him!" I cry. My panic spills over until my wheezing breaths catch in my chest and I brace both hands on the table. Murphy rests his head on my thigh. The warmth and weight are enough to pull me back from the brink, but just barely. It takes Wyatt's hand on the back of my neck and several minutes before I can form even a single word.

Swallowing hard, I meet his gaze. "Simon Arrens is the leader of the biggest human trafficking operation in the western United States. Thousands of barely legal men and women are brought in over the Mexican and Canadian borders every year, all put to work for him in one brothel or another. He owns more than a hundred of them. There are dozens in each of the major cities, and he gets away with it because he has police *and* FBI on his payroll. If he ever finds me..." I can't go on. I don't want to think about what he'll do.

Wyatt's chair tips over. The *bang* as it hits the floor makes me jump. "Hope. Were you...?" His voice fades, and Murphy paces between the two of us, nosing my hand then Wyatt's hip.

"No." I cradle my injured arm, and the memory card under my breast digs into my skin. "I'm thirty-six, Wyatt. The girls age out of the brothels at twenty-five or so—if they don't die first. I was only...*his*...for three years. He had other plans for me."

"You are *not* his." His growl sends goosebumps racing down my spine. I didn't know men like him—men who simply exude protectiveness—existed outside of romance novels, but here he is, standing less than ten feet away from me.

"I was," I whisper. "What else would you call it? I couldn't leave the compound. I didn't have a phone. A computer with internet access. A car. Money. Even a driver's license. He kept me prisoner. Just because he didn't sell me doesn't mean I wasn't his."

Wyatt stares at me, a muscle in his jaw ticking and anger vibrating off him in waves. I don't know what to do—how to make him understand. So I start talking.

"I met him in Vegas three and a half years ago while I was on vacation. He was charming. I was living in Los Angeles, and he actually *courted* me. Like flowers and candy delivered to my apartment, dates—he'd fly from Salt Lake City to L.A. on a private jet and whisk me away for a long weekend in Cancun or Vancouver..."

Now I actively regret not taking Wyatt up on the offer of bourbon. Though with how little I've eaten—for years as Simon kept me rail-thin—it would have gone right to my head.

"But every time we went somewhere, he'd disappear for hours on end. Business to take care of. And he was so sincere, so apologetic when he'd come back, that I believed him."

"What kind of business?" Wyatt braces his hands on the counter behind him. Still tense, but listening.

"Importing and exporting fine art. At least that's what he said. I should have questioned him. He never took me to a single gallery." With a sigh, I lift my gaze. "Will you sit down? Please?"

"Will you eat more?" he challenges.

I shoot him a look, but he's completely serious, and I roll my eyes. "I'll try."

Righting the chair, he perches on the edge of it, then slides my plate directly in front of me.

A deal's a deal, so I try a bite of potatoes. "You're not a terrible cook, you know." A slight flush darkens his cheeks. He's clearly not used to anyone flattering him. "These are really good."

"Use enough butter, anything can be tasty."

I don't know how I can laugh when I'm reliving my worst nightmares, but I do, and pain snakes around my torso. Wyatt reaches for my arm, but stops with his fingers hovering an inch away. "Fuck, Hope. I want to touch you, but—"

"It's all right," I say softly. I need him to anchor me to the present. He drapes his hand over my wrist, his fingers warm and strong. He starts to trace a pattern on my skin with his thumb. It's so calming, I melt against the back of the chair. "I know you're not him, Wyatt. He was never...tender. Hell, once he knew he *owned* me, he didn't speak to me at all unless he needed something." Too many memories battle for space in my head. Tension grabs the back of my neck. I'm still ravenously hungry, but the idea of more food turns my stomach.

Just get it out. All of it. Then maybe...you'll feel better.

"We dated for six months, and then out of the blue, the First Bank of Salt Lake City called me and offered me a job. It was more money than I'd ever made before, and when I told Simon, he was convinced it was kismet."

Wyatt snorts. "I take it he arranged for the job?"

I nod, my eyes burning. "Three weeks after I moved, they fired me. I'd rented an apartment, but my landlord was at my door the next day. No job, no lease. And Simon was right there. Offering me a place to stay, telling me he loved me and he'd been about to ask me to move in with him anyway. I was all alone. He'd already cut me off from my friends—insisting they were all talking behind my back. My mom is still in California, but we haven't spoken since I was a kid. She cheated on my dad when I was eight and left. Didn't even get in touch when I sent word that he died. I never forgave her for that."

The weight of how very alone I am hits me square in the chest. "Simon moved me into his house—his compound—but he sent almost all of my things to storage. Everything but my clothes. He said it would be easier for me to start fresh. I was so upset over losing my job that I believed him. God. I was so stupid."

"No. You weren't stupid, darlin'. You didn't do anything wrong. This Simon Arrens is a piece of shit who doesn't deserve to keep breathing."

Arguing won't get me anywhere. It doesn't matter that he's wrong. That it *was* my fault. That I didn't see the signs until it was too late. All I care about now is keeping Wyatt safe. But the only way to do that is to leave as soon as the storm lets me.

Wyatt

With every word that spills from her lips, Hope loses a little more of her strength, her spirit. She swipes at a single tear trailing down her cheek. "I *let* myself be trapped. No friends, no job. And it was okay for a few weeks. He had *staff*. I didn't have to lift a finger. His chef cooked all our meals—and I didn't protest when Simon insisted we both switch to this strict vegetarian diet. I was hungry all the time, but he told me I'd get used to it. And I did. Mostly."

I'll cook her bacon and steak every meal. Hell, I'll learn to bake. Cakes, cookies, pie. Anything she wants. Except, she's going to leave in a day—maybe two—and then she'll be alone again.

"Eat more, darlin'. Please." I nudge the plate closer, and she picks up her fork and pushes the mashed potatoes around in a circle before taking a single bite.

"I used to sneak veggies from the fridge," she admits. "Until he caught me. 'So that's why you're still so *plump*,' he said. 'I'm so disappointed in you, Hope. I thought you loved me.'" Her tone bleeds anger, but it's not all for the asshole who abused her. She's mad at herself too. I'm going to rip his balls off and feed them to him for how he stripped her down to nothing.

"The first time he hit me, it was close to midnight." She shudders, her gaze unfocused as she stares out the kitchen window into the darkness. "He'd taken my cell phone. To *upgrade* it. But it had been two days, and he hadn't given me a new one. So I went into his office and got online to order one for myself. When he found me, he was livid. He dragged me up to the bedroom, shoved me against the wall, and told me I was never to touch his things without permission again."

I clench my fists under the table. Murphy whines next to me and rests his head on my thigh.

Yeah, pal. I know. I need to calm the fuck down.

"I called him an asshole." Hope's shoulders curl inward, and she stares down at her plate. "That's when he backhanded me. I didn't even realize what had happened. One minute I was yelling at him, the next, I was on the floor tasting blood."

If I thought she'd let me, I'd take her in my arms. But she's trapped in her memories, and I know better than most the only way out is through.

"Simon apologized, tucked me into bed, and told me he loved me. He was so sweet, it confused the hell out of me. It was late. I couldn't leave. The next morning, I walked out to the main road with just my purse and hailed a cab to the airport. But when I got there..." Hope's eyes fill with tears, and she swallows hard. "None of my credit cards worked."

"Goddamn asshole." The urge to pace, to escape into the darkness, to take my aggressions out on the logs waiting to be split is strong, but Hope looks over at me like my presence is the only tether she has to sanity.

"A week before, he'd convinced me to let his financial advisor manage my portfolio. I didn't think twice about handing over all of my account information. I had almost a hundred and twenty-thousand tied up in investments. Maybe ten thousand liquid cash. He took everything." Her tears spill over, and I barely manage to move her plate out of the way in time.

Sliding closer, I wrap my arms around her and let her cry. "You didn't do anything wrong, darlin'."

"Bullshit," she whispers, her lips close to my ear. "I let him take everything from me. I should have called one of my friends from the airport. Or one of my former coworkers. Or even the police back in L.A." After a sniffle, she draws back. "Instead, when he showed up all 'knight-in-shining-armor' and told me it had to be some sort of mistake—that we'd sort it out—I believed him."

Hope wraps her arms around herself and sniffles. Exhaustion darkens circles under her eyes, and I don't think she has much left in her. "How long were you...*with* him?"

Her little huff is oddly reassuring. "I was only *with* him for maybe three weeks after that. But that's all the time he needed to trap me. Before yesterday, I hadn't left his compound in thirty months, two weeks, and five days."

Fuck. I'm going to end the shitstain. Painfully.

"Hope, look at me." Cupping her cheek, I dash away one last tear. "He can't hurt you here. You were heading to Seattle, right?" She nods, and I try for a reassuring smile. Not sure if I'm doing it right since I haven't had the need for that particular expression since I moved up here. "I know people there. They can protect you."

Her shoulders tense. "You don't understand. Maybe if I'd left right away, he'd have let me go. But after he knew I couldn't run—after he took all my money—he told me I had to 'earn my keep.' I used to manage tax accounts for multi-million dollar corporations. So I started doing his books. That's when he knew he *owned* me and stopped hiding what he did for a living."

Every new revelation ratchets my anger another dozen notches. "So you can put him away. Testify."

"Worse. Or better, depending on how you look at it." Hope fumbles for the belt on my robe. What the hell is she doing? With her good arm, she reaches down her shirt and winces. "I knew no one would believe me if I walked into a police station and claimed Simon Arrens was a criminal." She holds out her hand, and resting in her palm is a memory card.

"You have proof."

"Bank records, emails, his electronic ledgers...all of it. And he probably knows it. His laptop will have a record of the files I copied. The type of man he is? He'll be livid that I *dared* to leave him. But there's no way he'll let anyone with this data live free. He wants this back, and he'll kill anyone standing in his way."

7

Wyatt

For the first time since I turned my back on society, I regret it. Up here in the middle of nowhere, without a laptop or a cell phone—or any service—we can't call for help. Can't access what's on the memory card or find out if it even still works.

"I hid it in my bra," Hope says softly. "I didn't know if I'd be able to get out after I copied his ledgers. I thought...that would be one of the few places he wouldn't look. Even if he...punished me."

Fuck me. I don't want to know what the asshat did to punish her. The memory of her scarred back flashes through my mind, and I dig my fingers into my palms so hard I'm going to leave bruises. He whipped her. Used her as a punching bag. Maybe worse.

"That's why you wanted your bra earlier." Regret leaves a bitter taste in my mouth. I was so short with her over the damn thing. "To make sure the card was still there."

She nods, then glances back toward the couch. Her lower

lip wobbles slightly. "I didn't want to tell you. Not any of it. But the SUV...I'm sure Simon knows where it is. It was brand new."

"With GPS." Shit. "I found you two miles from here. But the car fell to the bottom of the ravine when the tree gave way. That's at least another half a mile. Unless this guy is the Abominable Fucking Snowman, there's no way he can get here until the snow melts. And that won't be for at least a day."

Hope doesn't respond. Her gaze is fixed on the memory card in my hand.

"Come with me, darlin'." I help her up and keep my arm around her waist as I lead her into the bedroom. "We're going to put this somewhere safe so you can relax."

She gives me the side eye. "I'm not just leaving it in your nightstand drawer, Wyatt."

"Not what I was suggesting." Pulling a painting of snow-covered mountains off the wall, I show her the safe, then press my index finger to the sensor. The door pops open, revealing two shelves, perfectly organized. My Glock 19, along with ammunition, a small stack of velvet boxes with all the medals and awards I'll never wear again, my Trident, and a folder of government papers one needs, but never actually uses.

Keying in the long sequence of numbers that lets me add a new print to the lock, I gesture to the sensor. "Right index finger."

"You're giving me access to your safe?" Confusion furrows her delicate brows. "You barely know me."

I lift her hand and press her finger to the glass square. "Hope, I was trained to read people. To know when they're lying and when they're not. Everything you just shared with me? I believe you, and there's no fucking way I'm going to let you deal with this alone. So put the memory card in the safe, and tomorrow, we'll go to the General Store, get you some clothes that actually fit, and I'll call one of the few men in this world I trust. West lives in Seattle. He and his team—they're all former military—can make sure Simon never hurts you again and keep you safe until he's been neutralized."

"N-neutralized?" Hope takes a step back, her voice cracking. "What do you mean?"

"Exactly what you think I mean. Men like that...prison doesn't stop them. Threats only make them more determined. Sometimes, there's no other way."

Fear steals the color from her cheeks, and she holds her injured arm close. "I used to pray he'd just...die. Or that one of his rivals would come for him. Even if that meant I died too." She shakes her head, tears glistening in her eyes. "But *I* never wanted to be responsible."

"You won't be."

"In what universe?" Holding up the memory card, she chokes back a sob. "I wanted him in jail. Somewhere he couldn't hurt me."

"And how did you expect that to work?" I arch my brows, and when she doesn't have an answer, I pluck the card from her hand and put it on the second shelf. "There is no place he can't get to you. Not if he's as connected as you say he is. If he has FBI agents on his payroll, he won't spend more than a single night behind bars. Men like that have contingency plans in place if anyone dares come after them. You're a financial planner. You deal in numbers. In black and white. I don't. I live in the gray—or I used to. *This?* This is firmly in the gray. You want to survive? See another Christmas? Another birthday? Be able to walk down the street without constantly looking over your shoulder? This is what needs to happen."

Slamming the safe door, I set the lock and rehang the painting.

Hope's strength, her defiance, and the shred of control she was holding onto crumble into dust, and she backs up until she hits the bed. "I can't... He'll never stop..." Covering her face with her hands, she breaks, her shoulders heaving with each silent sob.

Did you have to be so fucking blunt? This is why you're better off alone.

I don't know how to comfort her. Or if she'll even let me. I told her the truth, but that's not what she needed. Hope needed me to protect her. To reassure her. Before I can sink down next to her, Murphy pads into the room, jumps up onto the bed, and presses his whole body to hers. Taking a seat on her other side, I drape my arm around her. Hope curls into me, and fuck. It's the most natural thing in the world to have her in my arms. Every moment I spend with her makes me want more, and I'd do anything to stop her tears—except lie about the danger she's in.

"Shhh. It's gonna be okay." I'm not sure I believe my own words. How can I when I know so little about this Arrens shithead? But there's one thing I do know. He's not getting to her when I'm around.

She peers up at me. Splotched cheeks, red-rimmed eyes, her lip quivering—desperate for reassurance I don't know how to give. "How? You're right. He's too powerful."

"I have some damn powerful friends of my own, Hope. Friends who don't mind getting their hands dirty."

She doesn't look like she believes me, and fuck if I don't want to promise her I'll die before I let her ex-turned-captor hurt her again. I need to get the hell out of here. Put some space between us so I can think straight.

"We're safe for tonight. No one's getting through all that snow. It's late, and you're exhausted. I need to change your dressing, then you should rest."

She doesn't protest when I push to my feet and head for the kitchen for the first aid kit. And then I see her half-full dinner plate. Dammit.

I stop to pull another pound of bacon out of the freezer.

She's going to regain her strength if it's the last thing I do. I'm not sure how many more meals I'll have with her, but I'm gonna make them count.

By the time I return to the bedroom, Hope's already under the covers, fast asleep. My robe is draped across the end of the bed, and Murphy's curled up next to her.

Setting the first aid kit on the nightstand, I lean down and ghost my lips over her forehead. "Sleep well, darlin'. I'll change that dressing in the morning."

Before I cross the threshold back to the living room, I pause, one hand braced on the door jamb. "Never thought I'd say this, but I'm gonna miss you when I have to let you go."

Hope

I rise up on an elbow, blinking hard at the dull, orange glow coming from the small wood stove in the corner of the room. My arm aches, but it wasn't the pain that woke me.

Murphy's solid weight is gone, and only a hint of his warmth remains next to me. He whines from the next room, the sound immediately followed by a deep moan.

Wyatt.

Shit. I scramble to my feet, but the room spins. Throwing my hand out, I catch the wall and force myself to breathe.

"Take cover!" Wyatt's muffled shout—and the overwhelming pain in his voice—helps me focus, and I stumble out of the bedroom. Murphy stands in front of the couch, nosing Wyatt's shoulder. He whines again, finally pawing at the man's leg. But Wyatt fights against the blanket tangled around his hips.

"Wyatt? Wake up. You're scaring me." I lean down, my hand

inches from his shoulder until Murphy grabs the loose flannel next to my knee and tries to pull me back.

Wyatt sits up with a shout, fists clenched. His wild swing misses me by only a few inches, and I yelp.

Only Murphy's solid weight against my legs keeps me from falling over, and I start to shake.

"Fuck." Wyatt runs his fingers through his hair and groans. "*Never* wake me up from a nightmare, Hope. It's too dangerous."

Murphy pads over to him, whines, then jumps onto the couch until Wyatt puts his arms around the dog and buries his face in his soft brown fur. "Sorry, pal. I'm okay."

He repeats the words like it's the only way he'll believe them himself while I run back to the bedroom and hide under the covers.

"Don't embarrass me in front of a client again. Ever!" Simon punches me in the side, and when I double over, he grabs my hair and drags me down the hall to the tiny, windowless suite in the center of the second floor. A bed, small dresser, and a quarter bath—just a toilet and sink—fill the space, but the defining feature? The padlock on the outside of the door.

"No! Please! I'll be good. I promise." I struggle to pry his fingers from my hair, but he's too strong.

"If you cost me this deal, you're never leaving the house again." Shoving me face first against the wall, he yanks the thin straps of my dress down my arms, baring my back. His belt buckle jingles, and he snarls, "Don't move."

Tears stream down my cheeks. I know what's coming. How much it'll hurt. How I'll have to sleep on my stomach for a week. He saves the belt for special occasions, and apparently, my defiant refusal to eat what he claims is a delicacy—a thousand-year-old egg that smells like garbage—is a special occasion.

"Ten lashes for your attitude and another ten for wasting such an expensive meal."

The first strike steals my breath, and I bite my tongue so hard it bleeds. I won't give him the satisfaction of hearing me beg. But after the ninth time the belt hits my flesh, I can't help it.

"Hope!" The deep voice isn't *his*. The strong hands cupping my cheeks are calloused, but gentle. He smells like the outdoors. Like *Irish Spring* and wood smoke. The soft light from the fire highlights the deep lines around Wyatt's lips. "Come back to me, darlin'. You're safe."

The taste of blood makes me gag, and I cower away from him, still trapped in my memories. "I'll be good. I promise." Sobbing garbles my pleas, and all I want is to get out. Somewhere *he* can never find me.

"Murphy! Protect."

The words cut through the haze clouding my thoughts, and then a solid, warm weight presses against me. The cold nose to my jaw shocks me enough to take the edge off my panic, and I wrap my good arm around the dog, even though I'm still not sure where I am. "Stop. Please..." I whisper, and Murphy makes a reassuring sound.

The mattress dips, and I cry out. I can't move. Can't let him see everything. How scared I am. How I can't take another beating. How I'm so broken, there's nothing of *Hope* left.

Wyatt

Fucking hell. Hope's shaking, holding onto Murphy like he's her lifeline. And it's my fault.

The nightmare was nothing out of the ordinary. Pinned down in the middle of a blast zone, knowing CENTCOM was gonna blow the whole place in under five minutes, and our radio in pieces. We got out, but just barely.

"Hope? Do you know where you are?" She's wrapped

around Murphy, rocking back and forth with the occasional whimper.

"Y-yes."

I don't believe her. Not with her eyes screwed shut and her shoulders hiked up around her ears. "Not good enough, darlin'. Be more specific."

Hope blinks up at me, then relaxes her death grip on Murphy. "Your cabin. I'm sorry, Wyatt. I—"

"Don't apologize." The words sound too much like an order. Too harsh, too rough, and I swear under my breath. "You didn't do anything wrong. I did. I'm not used to having anyone around."

Peering at me like she still expects me to yell at her, she asks, "Does that happen every night?"

I reach over and stroke a hand down Murphy's back. "The nightmares? Most nights. But Murphy knows how to handle it. He keeps me from waking up like I did...with you. It's been months since I had that strong a reaction."

"Why tonight?" She's more curious than scared now, thank God. The guilt still threatens to pull me under, but I can fight it as long as Hope's okay.

"Got too far into it. Murph was a little preoccupied." I try for a smile, hoping she doesn't take my words for anything other than fact. "He was sleeping in here with you." Leaning closer to the dog, I touch my forehead to his. "Good boy." He swipes his tongue over my cheek once, then wriggles until he's next to Hope again. "I'll head back to the couch. Try to get some rest."

As I push to my feet, she reaches for my hand. "Don't go."

"What?" She can't mean that. I scared the poor woman so badly, she was begging me to stop. Or begging *him* to stop. And now she wants me to stay?

"For three years, I barely spoke to anyone. There was this one woman...one of Simon's housekeepers." She sniffs and swipes at her cheek. "Bettina. She was the only person who ever risked helping me after one of his...punishments. But only if Simon was away. If no one could see us. She helped me escape, and I'm sure he killed her for it." Hope's words dissolve into sobs, and I risk edging closer.

Resting my palm at the small of her back, I rub small circles. "He won't get away with it, darlin'. I'll make sure of that."

"You can't stop him." She tips her head up to look at me, and the heartbreak in her gaze kills me. "Tomorrow, I'll leave. But tonight...please. Stay with me?"

God. I want to. With everything I am. "I could hurt you, Hope. If I have another nightmare, you're better off sleeping alone."

"I was always alone when I was...*his*. Well, almost always." Her voice drops to a whisper, and she stares down at Murphy. "Simon expected sex twice a week."

The rage burning inside me demands to be released, but I have to stay calm. I'm so close to losing my shit and punching the wall, and I'm afraid that'll send Hope over the edge into a deep, dark abyss she'll never be able to climb out of.

"Did he *force* you?" I grit out.

"I didn't say no." She tangles her fingers in Murphy's fur, and he lies across her legs in full comfort mode. "But that's because there wasn't a point. I couldn't escape. Simon has a dozen men on his security team and cameras everywhere. I didn't have a phone, a driver's license, credit cards...nothing. It took me a year, stealing a couple of dollars at a time, to save enough for gas to get me from Salt Lake City to Seattle. It was all in the SUV. What was left, anyway."

Promising Hope I wouldn't go after this Simon asshole? Big mistake. Because I'm going to break every bone in his body. Ending with his neck. Right after I cut off his balls and shove them down his throat.

I swallow hard over the lump in my throat. "If you didn't have a choice, it's still—"

"I know." Hope glances up at me briefly, her eyes shimmering in the firelight. "But it was always quick. He wasn't...rough. Not in the bedroom. You've heard the phrase 'wham, bam, thank you, ma'am'?" She chokes back a sound that's half sob, half laugh. "Two minutes. Tops. Then he'd send me back to my room in the other wing of the house. He knew I was clean—despite his business, he never touched the girls at the brothels—and I wouldn't fight him. Once in a while, he'd demand I dress up and let him parade me around in front of his business associates. His obedient little number cruncher who hid all his dealings from the government. But even then he barely spoke to me."

A tear rolls down her cheek, and I ease closer so I can brush it away with my knuckle. "I'll stay, Hope. I'll sleep on the floor. Just let me get a blanket and pillow."

When I return, she pulls back the blankets and stares pointedly at the empty side of the bed. "Come here. Please."

Fuck me. This is a bad idea of epic proportions. But she needs this. It's written all over her face. And maybe...I do too.

"Push over, Murph." I snap my fingers, and the dog moves to the foot of the bed, curling up at Hope's feet. We're two fully clothed adults, and I can make it through the next few hours lying next to her. Even if I have to count the beams on the ceiling a hundred times. Because up close, her scent and her warmth do things to me that will make sleep damn near impossible.

8

Wyatt

SUNLIGHT SLICES through a gap in the thick drapes, waking me from the best night's sleep I've had in months. I thought being close to Hope would keep me up all fucking night. Instead, I was out in minutes.

From the angle of the beam hitting me in the face, it has to be close to nine. I haven't slept in this late since before I joined the Navy.

Hope curls against me, wrapped in my arms with her head tucked under my chin. Like she belongs there. I've never felt so at peace. So...whole.

At the foot of the bed Murphy peers up at me with a look that clearly says, "*Can we do this every night?*"

Unsurprising since he's usually relegated to his own bed on the floor.

She hasn't stirred, and I revel in these last few minutes I have with her. The slow, *drip, drip, drip* of the snow melting from the eaves is a sure sign we'll be able to make it to the General Store by lunch time. But until she wakes up, I'm going to hold her and memorize every single thing about her. Her hair tickling my cheek. The way her leg hooks over mine. The softness of her breasts through my t-shirt.

There's no fucking way I'm going to be able to hand her off to West and just...*leave.* Not that I have any idea what I *can* do.

Move back to a city? No way in hell. And I'm damn sure not going to ask a woman who just escaped a *three-year-long* abusive relationship to stay here—in the middle of nowhere—with a man she's only just met.

Her little moan sends blood rushing to my dick. I try to scoot away, but Hope drapes her arm around my waist and snuggles against me tighter.

"Wyatt?"

Her voice is a hundred times sexier first thing in the morning. "I'm right here, darlin'." I skim my lips over the shell of her ear, and goosebumps race along her skin.

"You're real." With a sigh, she rests her head on my chest. Murphy leaps off the bed, heading for the kitchen—and the custom doggie door in the basement.

"Real?" I ask, pulling the blankets up against the chill in the room. The wood stove needs tending, but hell if I'm going to miss out on a second of closeness with Hope to do it. Not yet. "I'm one hundred percent real, darlin'. Can't you feel my arms around you?"

Her legs tangle with mine, and it doesn't matter that we're fully clothed. I'm hard as a fucking rock for her. From the way she moves, how her hips swivel against me, she's not entirely unaffected. "It's been so long since I had...this. Someone to hold me. Someone I can hold back."

Words fail me. The sorrow in her voice raises a lump in my throat. She's been through so much, and yet she's still here. That bastard didn't kill her spirit. It might be bruised. Weak. Beaten. But she survived, and that's a fucking miracle.

"I'll hold you as long as you want. Or at least until nature calls for one of us." The quip has the desired effect, and Hope huffs out a laugh, then relaxes again.

Delicate fingers skate over my t-shirt, tracing the ridges of my abs. No one's touched me like this in years. I didn't know how much I'd missed human contact. Holed up in the middle of nowhere with only Murphy for company *sounded* like a good idea. Even felt like one. Until yesterday. Now, I'd give anything to be closer to Seattle. Closer to West and his team. Closer to anywhere the woman in my arms might want to settle.

With a sigh, Hope tucks a lock of dark hair behind her ear. "Wyatt, I'm scared. Simon *will* find me. And if I can't send him to prison—or if that doesn't stop him—he'll..." She chokes back a sob, then buries her face in the blankets. "He probably won't kill me. But he'll make me wish I were dead."

The growl escapes before I can stop it, and she flinches against me.

"He won't hurt you again, Hope. The guy I told you about—West?—is a friend from BUD/S." She peers up at me, confusion wrinkling her dark brows. "It's the training you have to go through before you can become a SEAL. West works with a whole group of Black Ops guys now, and the team leader owes me a favor. A big one."

As long as I live, I'll never forget the sight of Ryker McCabe crawling out from under a snow-covered bush eight clicks from Hell Mountain. Son of a bitch walked almost five miles barefoot, malnourished, and half-dead before we found him. Then tried to turn around and lead us back to his brother-in-arms, Dax Holloway, who was still trapped in the Taliban's most notorious prison.

"Simon has people everywhere," Hope whispers. "What if your friend—or one of the men he works with—is—"

"Not a chance in hell," I grit out. "West Sampson would slice off his own nuts and toss 'em into the deep fryer before he'd let *anyone* get their hooks into him."

Her gaze holds mine, and silence stretches between us until Hope finally nods. "Will I ever see you again? After I go with West?" The pure need in her eyes mirrors what I feel every time I breathe in her scent. Touch her. Talk to her.

"I don't know." It's the truth, as much as I hate to admit it. "I can't come with you to Seattle. Me and cities? We don't get along. And you sure as shit can't stay here."

Her expression hardens, and anger has her shoving at my chest with her good arm. "You can be a real ass, Wyatt—"

"Fuck. That's not what I meant." Pinning her with my arm around her back, I wait for the huff I know is coming. Followed by a scowl. "Will you let me explain?"

"Fine." She rolls her eyes, but some of the tension melts from her limbs.

"I live in a seven-hundred square foot cabin in the middle of nowhere, Hope. No phone. No TV. No Netflix or internet. The fanciest meal I can make is grilled trout—if it's nice enough to go fishing. The only vehicle I own is an ATV. If I want to leave the mountain, I gotta call West. And hope he has time to drive almost five hours to get here."

A little of the light leaves Hope's gaze with every word out of my mouth. I should stop, but I need her to understand.

"You went through hell and came out the other side. You deserve to live where you can do whatever you want. Go to a movie, order pizza, make friends. You can't do any of those things up here."

She chews on her lip, and even though she's been here less than forty-eight hours, I can read her easily. She's made up her mind about something.

"What is it, darlin'?" I should stop with the term of endearment. Every time I say it, I want more with this woman than I have any right to expect. But whether it's the way she clings to me or the flashes of strength and sass she finds despite what she's been through, I'm falling for her.

"I haven't felt safe for three years, Wyatt." The desperation in her tone stirs every protective instinct I have. "Until now."

Pride swells in my chest until I realize *I* had nothing to do with it. "You felt safe with six feet of snow outside this door. And Murphy sleeping next to you."

"No." Sitting up, Hope reaches for my hand and links our fingers. "Murphy's great. And yes, the snow helped. But you're the one who pulled me out of the car. Who patched me up. Fed me. Protected me. And held me all night."

I want to tell her that was a mistake. But I wouldn't take it back. I'll cherish the memory of Hope in my arms for the rest of my days. "I thought I was better off alone. But having you here.... It makes me want what I can't have." The admission costs me, but Hope deserves the truth. Leaning closer, I drag a knuckle along her jaw, and she holds her breath.

The ache to pull her against me, to claim those full lips and make her moan rears up, and she melts into my arms. But then bold, brave Hope takes over, shocking me, and making my dick rocket to attention.

It's *her* tongue that begs for entrance, not mine. I yield—I'd do anything for her in this moment. Two hard points of her nipples call to be pinched, and when I roll one between my thumb and forefinger, Hope mewls into the kiss.

I slide a hand from her hip to her waist, then higher so I can cup the gentle swell of her breast. Hope shudders, and all I can think about is getting her naked. About her begging me to taste her.

Warning bells go off in my head. This is dangerous on an epic level. I'm broken in so many ways. Then again, maybe Hope is too. Maybe that's why we fit.

"Hope," I manage when I finally break off the kiss. "We should stop."

Her cheeks flush bright pink, and her fingers dig into my ass. "I need this."

What?

Clearly, I've lost my poker face in all the months living alone, because she huffs and slides off my lap. "Don't look so shocked. I'm allowed to want things."

"I...shit. Of course you are. But—"

"My life hasn't been my own for three years, Wyatt. I didn't get to pick what I wanted to eat. What I wore. What time I got up in the morning. I didn't get sick days or vacation time or anything that couldn't be taken away in a heartbeat."

She scoots to the edge of the bed and swings her legs over the side. Despite almost dying two days ago, she stands easily and turns to me. "By tomorrow, I'll be safe, sure. According to you, anyway. But I won't be free. Right now? I'm free. I thought you'd understand."

The sadness in her eyes steals my breath. Before I can find my words, she slips into the bathroom and locks the door.

9

Hope

WALKING AWAY from Wyatt feels wrong. My heart pounds half out of my chest, and I'm so turned on, I can't think straight. Until I turn my gaze to his bathtub.

It's every woman's fantasy. Deep enough for me to sink into hot water up to my neck. After I start the tap, I strip out of his clothes. Did he wash mine last night? I fell asleep so quickly after dinner, I have no idea. The idea of wearing the clothes Simon bought me—clothes that had my blood all over them—makes my skin crawl.

And then I hear his voice in my memories.

"You need a new wardrobe, my sweet," Simon announces as he breezes into the bedroom, several garment bags draped over his arm. "I took the liberty. Change into something more...appropriate before dinner."

Unzipping one bag after another, I find nothing but silk, cashmere, and linen. No jeans. No sweatshirts. Two of the staff rush in, one carrying four shoe boxes, the other making a beeline for my closet.

My jaw drops as they proceed to toss everything I own into the laundry cart. "Stop! What are you doing?" I snatch my UCLA sweatshirt out of Bettina's hands and clutch it to my chest.

"Your wardrobe is abhorrent. You will not wear that *and be seen with me." Simon tries to take the sweatshirt from me, but I hold tight. "Hope..."*

"No. Not this one. I won't wear it out of the house. Or where anyone can see me. Please..." Tears prick at my eyes. How much more can he take from me? Sure, I have my own bedroom—complete with a luxurious en-suite bath and thousand thread-count sheets, but he won't let me leave the house, drive his cars, doesn't want me to work unless it's for him, and now...this?

"Fine. You may keep that one. But you are not to leave this room wearing it. Hurry up and change. Dinner is in ten minutes."

The cabin door slams, pulling me from my memories, and I scramble to turn off the faucet before sinking into the tub with a moan. This is pure heaven. With my injured arm draped over the side, I settle deeper so the hot water can soothe all my sore muscles.

Wyatt moves around in the next room, heavy footsteps and his deep voice—talking to Murphy, I assume—reassuring. Even if I am frustrated with him.

I didn't realize how much I needed to be touched. How much I'd missed it. Not until Wyatt held me all night.

Even before he trapped me, Simon was never tender. We kissed. Had sex. Held hands in public—when he used to let me leave the house. But he never stroked my cheek. Never rubbed my back. Never cuddled. He preferred using his fists.

Wyatt is his opposite in every way. He doesn't have the smooth, perfect words. For all his swagger and physical strength, he's awkward as hell around me. Like he's constantly worried he's going to say the wrong thing.

Oh, shit. He is.

I sit up so quickly, a few drops of water splash onto the floor.

Everything makes sense now. Has he ever had a girlfriend? Been close to anyone he didn't serve with? I need to ask him.

When the water starts to cool, I wrap myself in a thick, dark blue towel. Washing the blood out of my hair in the sink takes all the energy I have left, and by the time I pull on Wyatt's robe and trudge out to the kitchen, I'm practically shaking.

The only thing keeping me going? The delicious scents wafting from the stove.

"Is that more bacon?" I ask. "You're spoiling me." The room starts to spin, and I stumble, but Murphy's right there, leaning against my legs to help keep me upright.

"Hope! Dammit. I knew I shouldn't have left you alone." Wyatt's hands mold to my hips, and he's so close, his warmth seeps into me through the robe. "How bad is it?"

"I'm just a little dizzy. Nothing breakfast won't fix."

"Fucking hell," he mutters as he guides me to the table and pulls out a chair. "You need more than a plate of bacon and some eggs. You need a doctor."

Great. Grumpy, surly, closed-off Wyatt is back. The kind, gentle, warm man who held me all night and made me feel alive for the first time in forever went AWOL, and I don't know how to get him back.

Two hours later, after a mostly silent breakfast and a short nap, I'm dressed in my old clothes. They're clean, but in the light, I can still see the bloodstains. Outside the big front window, the snow sparkles in the sun, and water drips from the eaves.

Wyatt thrusts a large down jacket at me. "It'll take us twenty minutes to get to the General Store, but almost twice as long to get back. It's a steep climb back up the mountain."

Two of me could fit inside the coat, and despite the overly

large plate of bacon, eggs, and hashbrowns Wyatt served me this morning, I'm still shaky.

When he passes me a pair of gloves, his gaze zeroes in on my fingers still fumbling for the zipper. "Let me."

I hate this lingering weakness, and I huff, but then he's so close, I can smell his shampoo. He stills my hands with his, and for a moment, something almost magical sparks between us. I hold his dark, intense gaze, mesmerized, barely able to breathe. Something as simple as him bundling me into a coat shouldn't be so intimate. Yet, it is.

"Here," he says, snagging a fleece-lined hat from a hook by the door and offering it to me. "Put this on."

The moment shatters, and I scowl. "I really need *all* of this?"

Wyatt arches a brow. "Do you want to freeze to death?"

"Of course not. I tried that the other day and didn't enjoy it at all." I offer him a weak smile, but Wyatt's having none of it. His stern expression would scare me if it weren't for the heat in his eyes.

He tugs the ear flaps down and secures them under my chin, a move that should annoy me, but instead, is oddly tender. "Then you'll wear the hat. And the gloves."

I'd argue—because I've had it with men telling me what to do—but then Wyatt adds, "Please."

It's his tone that gets me. The worry. The care. The intense need to protect me. So I wear the gloves.

He pats his hip like he's checking for his wallet, but as he reaches for a small backpack, a leather holster peeks out from under his jacket.

"You're bringing a gun?" Panic claws at my chest, and I take a step back. Murphy whines and paws at my thigh. It barely takes the edge off. Until Wyatt's deep voice anchors me.

"Look outside." He waves his hand toward the window. The towering snow drifts have all but disappeared, and while it's still white as far as I can see, a light rain falls steadily. "It's warmer today. Which means..."

"Simon's men could be out there." A cold chill settles in my belly, despite the hat, coat, and gloves. "Is it safe for me to go with you?"

"You're sure as shit not staying here alone," he growls.

"Excuse me?" Despite my fear, I find a small bit of strength deep inside. With my back straight, I march over to him and get right in his face. As much as I can since he's at least six inches taller than I am. "You saved my life, brought me here, and now you don't trust me?"

"For fuck's sake." Wyatt pulls me close and cups the back of my neck. The kiss is rough. Demanding. Passionate. Definitely *not* a kiss born out of mistrust. I'm breathless when he lets me come up for air, but he doesn't release me. Instead, he cups my cheeks and urges me to meet his gaze. "You're not staying here alone because until I *know* you're safe and somewhere that bastard can never find you, I'm not letting you out of my sight."

Wyatt

With Hope's arms wrapped tightly around my waist, focusing on the hazardous terrain is a hell of a lot harder than it should be. The storm passed overnight, but the temperature still hovers just above freezing.

The top layer of snow has turned to ice, and wind stings my cheeks. I wish I had a spare set of goggles for Hope. Though without them, she presses her face to my back.

Not a terrible position to be in.

There are only a half dozen cabins on this particular mountain peak, and last time I bothered to check, mine was the only one occupied year round. No other tracks in the snow—thank fuck—but that could change any minute. If I wasn't worried about leaving a trail directly to my door, I'd hike all the way to the highway where the SUV left the road to see if anyone had been looking around.

Parker's General Store is a good five hundred feet lower in elevation than my cabin, and by the time I pull the ATV around the back of the building, a few patches of green peek through the snow.

Hope doesn't let go of me when I kill the engine, so I pat her hands gently. "We're here."

"I don't like ATVs," she mutters, pain tightening her voice.

Helping her off the back seat, I steady her until I can get a good look at her face. Shit. The ride wasn't good to her.

Her car fell halfway down the mountain two days ago. Of course she's in pain. Be a little more sensitive, dumbass.

"How many times have you ridden on one before today?" I ask.

"None." Her little huff is adorable. Full of exasperation and a hint of fear. "But shock absorbers would be nice."

"I'll buy you a cushion. Pretty sure Old Man Parker stocks those." Scanning our surroundings, I blow out a breath. The slush is almost pure white. If another vehicle had come and gone, it would be stained with mud.

The bell on the door jingles as we enter, and warm air rushes over us. Half a dozen rows of shelves are filled to overflowing. The General Store doesn't just sell groceries. The owner, Clarence, stocks most of the basics—frozen bread, powdered milk, eggs—as well as kerosene, candles, batteries, and some seasonally appropriate clothing. When I moved up here, he added dog food to the mix.

Parker's also has the only working phone for miles. Even internet when the weather's good. "Let me do the talking, darlin'. Keep the hat on and don't tell Clarence your name." With my arm around her waist, I guide her to the front counter.

"Wyatt? What the hell are you doing back here already? It's only been four days." The raspy voice carries from the back corner of the store, and Clarence shuffles out from his private office. "And who's this?"

Hope shrinks against my side, tension vibrating from every muscle.

"Old friend of mine. Came up for a visit and got trapped by that fucking blizzard. We need to use your phone and pick up a few things if that's okay."

Clarence looks me up and down. He's a former Marine, and his gaze lingers at my right hip. Just long enough. He knows I'm carrying. And lying through my teeth. To his credit, he only pauses a beat.

"The office is nice and toasty. Got the space heater running. Let me get my Sudoku book outta there and you can take all the time you need."

The man has to be well over seventy, and arthritis has stolen his speed, so while he retrieves his book of puzzles, I lead Hope to a shelf with folded t-shirts, sweatshirts, jeans, and a pitiful selection of men's and women's underwear. "I don't know shit about sizes, darlin'. But grab anything you think will fit."

She peers up at me through her lashes. "You don't need to buy me anything. I'm...fine."

"The hell you are. Anyone looks twice at that sweater, they're going to see the bloodstains. And you can't tell me you want to keep wearing clothes *he* bought you."

My words register like a slap to her face, and she hunches her shoulders. "Okay."

Fuck me.

"Hope, I'm sorry." Cupping her cheek, I skate my thumb over the fading bruise under her right eye. "You can wear whatever you want. I just thought you might be more comfortable—and warmer—with some new clothes. I can afford 'em. You live off the grid, you don't spend much money."

By the time Clarence is perched on his stool at the cash register, she has a sweatshirt, a blue and gray flannel shirt, and a pair of dark jeans clutched in her arms, along with a pack of panties and two pairs of socks. We leave the small pile at the counter while we use the phone.

"You're sure about this?" Hope asks when I close the door behind us. "That you can trust this guy you're calling?"

Wrapping my arms around her, I relish the way she relaxes into my embrace. I don't know how the hell I'm supposed to let her go, but I have to. "I trust him, darlin'. With my life."

"SAMPSON."

The familiar voice makes the corners of my lips twitch, even as a knot forms in my gut. "It's Wyatt."

"What's wrong?" The former SEAL team leader shifts into threat assessment mode seamlessly, which eases some of the tension gathering between my shoulder blades.

"I need an extraction. Not for me, but for an HVT with intel."

With every word, Hope's eyes grow wider. I lean against Clarence's desk and hold out my free hand until she links our fingers.

"Where?"

"My cabin. She's staying with me until you come to get her. And if you can't get here, you better send someone you trust with your life."

"Her?" The first hint of true surprise colors his tone, and I can practically *see* his eyebrows shoot up. "You want to tell me who *she* is and where *she* came from?"

"Not over an unsecured line, I don't. She's safe with me for now, but she won't be for long unless you can get her into WITSEC or take out the asshole who's after her. Your call."

"Hang on." Muffled conversation follows for a minute, and then he's back. "Checked the weather report. That storm is going to make it impossible to get there by car until close to noon tomorrow. I can get a bird and drop in—with or without my team—but that makes extraction a hell of a lot harder."

"Tomorrow's fine. The cabin's secure, and if you can't get here, neither can anyone else. We'll be waiting for you." Before he can end the call, I add, "West? I owe you for this, man."

"Family doesn't keep track of debts, Wyatt. You know that. See you tomorrow."

10

Hope

"SIMON? WHAT IS ALL THIS?" I ask, staring at the laptop screen. At rows and rows of ledger entries totaling millions of dollars. Each is marked with a code. MX-F. CA-M. TX-M. NV-F. States? Countries?

He leans down, caging me against the desk with his arms. I want to squirm. But that would make him angry, and the bruises on my arms still ache where he grabbed me and shook me two days ago.

"You've done an excellent job managing the finances for the art gallery, my sweet. But that's only one of my businesses. This is the other."

Thirty minutes later, my eyelids feel like sandpaper. I swipe at the tears that won't stop falling and peer up at him. "No, Simon. I won't be a part of this. Buying and selling people? *You're a monster."*

His palm connects with my cheek, so hard and fast, the fancy desk chair spins. I tumble to the floor. Pain sings up my arms. My knees ache where they hit the marble.

"You're a part of this already, Hope. How do you think I hide all this money? The art gallery cleans it for me. You *clean it for me."*

Oh, God. I cover my face with my hands, unable to stop the sobs wracking my body. I've helped him. All those young men and women he forces to work in his brothels across the western United States? I've helped him torture them. Trap them. Keep them.

"Stop the water works," he snarls. "Get to work or I will lock you in your room until you forget what the sun looks like."

"Hope?" Wyatt brushes his knuckles along the curve of my jaw, and I jerk back with a gasp. A plate—with a grilled cheese sandwich—lands on the table with a clatter, and his hand falls away. "Fuck. I'm sorry."

"You didn't do anything wrong," I say quietly, unwilling to meet his gaze. My stomach rumbles, and I swallow hard to force my memories into a tiny box where they can't hurt me. "That smells great."

He drops into the chair next to me with a sigh. "You haven't said a word since we got back."

No. Because all I can think about is how easy it would be for Simon to get to me. And you.

But I don't say any of that. Instead, I focus on the window. "The snow's melting." A few patches of green peek through the expanse of white outside the big picture window. "Are you sure he won't get here before your friend?"

"He'd have to find this place first. The snow would have hidden my tracks from where I found you, and this place isn't on any map, GPS, or satellite."

"How did you manage that?" Taking a bite of the sandwich, I try not to moan. God, I've missed carbs and butter and cheese so much. Even the fake, bright orange "cheese food" that makes the best sandwiches.

His lips twitch, about as close as he gets to a smile. "West. Or folks he knows, anyway. His wife designs security systems for big corporations. And Wren—she's married to Ryker, the head of the K&R firm—is a hacker. She keeps this place off of satellite scans." He runs a hand through his hair, his shoulders hunched and the hint of amusement in his expression gone in the blink of an eye. "I wanted to disappear, and they made it happen."

No one should ever *want* to disappear. Though I suppose *I* do. Or at least...I need to.

Reaching across the table, I drape my hand over his. "You're a good man, Wyatt. Why did you think you had to disappear?"

He doesn't answer. Just shakes his head and turns his whole focus to his plate. Dammit.

"You don't *look* like a coward," I say with a shrug.

"A coward?" Wyatt chokes down a bite of sandwich and clears his throat. "What the fuck, Hope?"

"Every time you get close to sharing something real with me, you shut down." Lifting my gaze, I find pain in his eyes, along with something else. Need? Loneliness? If only he'd tell me. "Tomorrow, I'll be gone. And all I want before I go is...you."

His chair scrapes over the polished wood planks, and then he's lifting me to my feet. When his lips slant over mine, I don't even try to hide how much I need him. My fingers find his belt, but he stops me before I can undo the buckle.

"Hope. This is a bad idea," he says, warning lending a rough edge to his voice. It doesn't scare me. *Wyatt* doesn't scare me. He makes me feel protected and warm and tingly all over.

"This—" I gesture between us, "—is the first thing I've wanted in a very long time that I can actually...have."

That's all it takes. Pulling off my ripped sweater to expose my bra, the most possessive growl rumbles in his chest. "You're never wearing *his* clothes again. I'll burn them if I have to."

After what I've been through the past three years, those words shouldn't turn me on, but they do. Because Wyatt will never hurt me. It's in his DNA. The very core of who he is. Honesty. Valor. And above all, honor.

"We can burn them. Later." Sliding my hand up to curl around his neck, I pull him closer. His kiss burns so hot, my clothes are in danger of catching fire all on their own. Strong arms wrap around me, holding me close.

With each bold stroke of his tongue, my need ratchets another dozen notches. His hard length grinds against me, and the sensations? I haven't felt anything like this in so long. My nipples harden to sharp nubs, and a flood of arousal dampens my panties.

"Bedroom," he manages, then scoops me up in one fluid motion. A grunt escapes his lips, but before I can ask him about it, we're moving, and he's kissing me again.

Setting me on the bed so I'm on my knees, he guides my uninjured arm around his neck. "Hold on to me, darlin'."

The order sends goosebumps racing up my bare arms. My pants cascade down my thighs, and he unhooks the bra. Embarrassment warms my cheeks at the bruises still healing across my ribs, but Wyatt doesn't seem to care, because he dips his head to suck a nipple into his mouth.

The shock is like a jolt of electricity straight to my core, and I cry out as my head falls back. His fingers dance over my mound, slipping under the edge of my panties to find me soaked. God. I could come from this alone.

"Wyatt...please," I beg, my legs shaking.

He pulls back to search my face, then smiles. Actually smiles. "Like that?"

Before I can answer, he eases me down, then sits next to me to pull off his boots. I expect him to strip off his shirt next, but he doesn't. Just shucks his jeans and straddles me.

His legs...God. They're huge, and the coarse hair tickles my thighs. When I try to slide my hands under the flannel to his back, he stops me, and I'm shocked to find fear in his eyes. "What's wrong?"

"Been through some shit. It's not...pretty. My shirt stays on."

Shoving at him, I wriggle until my back is against the headboard, then point at my hip bone. Four fingertip bruises are still painfully dark. Simon grabbed me from behind the day before I escaped. "And these are? What about the ones on my neck? Or the scars on my back? Those are permanent." Tears hover on my lower lids, lending a shimmer to everything around me. "I saw the tail end of your nightmare, remember? I know you're... damaged. So am I. Do you honestly think anything I find under there is going to matter to me?"

Without giving him a chance to respond, I start unbuttoning his shirt. His shoulders tense, but he doesn't protest, and I slide the flannel down his arms.

The corded muscles of his back flex under my fingers. "Hope..."

"You're perfect, Wyatt. I don't know what the heck you're—"

He turns, letting the shirt fall to the floor. His right arm bears a thick scar from his elbow to his shoulder. Across his chest, dozens of red marks, some the size of staples, others larger, blaze a trail down his side and disappear beneath his black briefs.

"What happened?" With a light touch, I trace the long-healed wounds, lean forward, and press my lips to the scar on his arm.

"Shrapnel."

I move until I can see his back, finding even more damage, but for the life of me, I can't imagine what he's ashamed of. Until he rises and tugs down his briefs. His cock stands at full mast, but the scars continue, interrupting the neatly trimmed dark hair below the *v* of his abs. "I don't—" Clearing my throat, I try again. "I don't know why you think you aren't...'pretty.' Though handsome, rugged, manly...those might all be better words."

Relief washes over him, and it brings such a change to his face he almost looks like a different person. One who isn't hiding anymore. At least not from me.

Wyatt

I never imagined I'd stand naked in front of a woman again. Especially not one I plucked out of a crashed car during a freak spring blizzard who's on the run for her life. But here we are.

Hope is everything I've ever wanted. And the one person I can never have. Not permanently. Not beyond tonight. But I'm damn sure going to make the most of the time we have left.

"Come here," Hope whispers, sliding back on the bed. Clad in only her panties, she beckons to me. I hook my thumbs in the black silk to slide them down her hips, and my God. The flush to her skin is so fucking beautiful.

Positioning myself between her thighs, I kiss my way from her left knee all the way up to her glistening pussy. I'm desperate to taste her, but I want to make this last. To make it a memory we can both hold on to for the rest of our days.

With a single swipe of my tongue to her folds, I pull a whimper from her lips, then continue my trail of kisses up between her breasts.

"Are you sure, darlin'?" Tipping my head up to meet her hooded gaze, I hold my breath. If she says no...it might kill me. But I'll walk away.

"Yes," she says, and the breathy tone to her voice makes me so hard, my dick *hurts*. But Hope's pleasure comes first.

My palms are rough against the soft skin of her inner thighs. We're opposites in every way. Yet she still wants me. "You're so fucking wet for me, Hope."

A sexy smile curves her lips. "Only for you."

I pause, my lips inches from her sweet scent. "*Only* for me."

Her taste could sate me for the rest of my life. Like the ocean after a storm. I blaze a slow trail through her velvet folds and relish the way her thighs tremble. Tracing patterns over her clit, I drink her in. Every touch, every flick of my tongue coils her muscles tighter. Her legs move restlessly, hands fisting in the sheets, and I slip a finger inside her.

"More," she begs.

I'll give her anything she asks for, so I add a second finger, pumping in and out while I find my rhythm with my tongue. Her little whimpers turn into moans punctuated with gasps, and I only stop long enough to ask, "Like this, do you?"

"God, yes," she breathes. "Don't...stop..."

I chuckle with my lips pressed to her pussy, and the motion has her back arching. Twisting my hand so I can find her g-spot, I curl my fingers and suck gently on her clit.

"Come for me, darlin'," I murmur against her. With one final whimper, she lets go.

Mine.

That's the only thought I can muster as Hope shudders in my arms. That this beautiful, brave, intelligent woman is mine, and I'll do anything to keep her safe. She came alive for me with each kiss, each touch, each tremor.

I have to let her go. Tomorrow, I *will* let her go. But not tonight. Tonight, I'm going to worship her until we're both too tired to move.

Her eyes are still closed, but she's wearing a dazed smile and clings to me when I pull the blankets up over us. "Wyatt?" she murmurs. "You don't think we're done, do you?"

"I'll never be done with you, darlin'."

Never? Watch your mouth, asshole. You don't deserve a forever with her. And she deserves a hell of a lot more than you can ever provide.

Hope wriggles out of my embrace and pushes up on an elbow. "Do you have a condom?"

Fuck me.

I stare down at the blanket bunched in my hands, unwilling—or unable—to meet her gaze. "No. I'm clean, darlin'. But all that shrapnel damage...the docs don't think I can have kids. They weren't sure, though. And I live alone. Never planned on seeing another soul outside of Clarence ever again. I'm sorry."

With a sigh, I roll off the bed—or try to—but she stops me, her fingers warm around my wrist. "I'm protected. I can't get pregnant. But..." Her cheeks flame bright red, and now she's the one who looks away.

"Simon demanded sex twice a week."

That shitstain touched her. He fucked her.

"He wore a condom." Her whisper is so quiet, I can barely make out her words, but when I tip her chin up, I know she's telling the truth. "Every time."

"Then come here." Lying back, I wait for her to climb on top of me. I'm still hard as a rock, and she wraps her hand around my shaft. "Fuck, Hope. You don't know what you do to me."

Her smile lights up the entire room until she leans down and swirls her tongue over my crown. My vision goes white. It's been so long. When I focus on her again, she's sucking me deep. My God. If she keeps this up, I won't last.

"Hope," I manage. "Stop."

She releases me with a little *pop* from her lips, and fear churns in her eyes. "Did I do something wrong?"

"Fuck, no. That was...amazing." I slide my arm around her waist and pull her closer. The position gives me access to her perfect breasts, and I pinch a nipple, rolling it between my fingers and thumb until she shudders and lets her head fall back. "I want to come inside you. That's all. Another few seconds of...*that*...and I'd be done for."

Soft, black locks smelling of my shampoo tickle the hand I brace along her spine. I want her to always smell like this. Feel like this. Leaning forward, I capture the other nipple between my teeth, sucking it, hard.

A blush races up her chest, all the way to her neck. I want to taste every fucking inch of her. Wrapping my arms around her, I tug her down to me, kissing from her shoulder to her neck and up to her ear. My teeth score the shell, and she whimpers my name.

"Are you ready, darlin'?"

"Uh huh." She's so wet, and my dick is already slick with precum. Fastening my hands around her hips, I help guide her. I don't remember the last time a woman rode me, but with Hope, I think this is what she needs—and wants—because the relief in her eyes is both reassuring and heartbreaking.

"Hope? Listen to me." Cupping her cheek, I focus on her. I want her to know she's my whole world—if only for tonight. "Nothing matters to me but you. Your happiness. Your safety. Your pleasure. If you want to stop, we stop. Just say the word."

"Wyatt. I want *this*. You. I'm not fragile. Not some flower with a broken stem you need to protect. I survived. I have a chance..." Her voice cracks, and she clears her throat. "A chance at a future. And I'm not wasting a second of it."

She positions herself right above my rigid cock and slowly, carefully, lowers herself on top of me.

"Fuck. You feel so damn good."

When she starts moving her hips, I'm a goner. I won't last long. Not after denying myself for years. Sure, I got it off in the shower from time to time, but this is a whole new ballgame.

With every minute we spend together, I fall harder. I want more than her body. I want her heart too.

Watching her? The light in her eyes is intoxicating. Her breasts bounce as she thrusts her hips, and a shy smile bends her lips at the corners.

"You're so damn beautiful."

I keep one hand on her waist and slide the other to her

mound, finding that hard, tight nub I know will send her flying over the edge once more. Hope cries out when I start to circle my thumb, and even more of her delicious scent washes over me.

I'm so close my heartbeat roars in my ears. "Fly with me, Hope."

And she does.

11

Hope

WITH A MUG of coffee warming my hands, I relax against the pillows. The rhythmic *thump, thump, thump* of Wyatt chopping wood outside threatens to lull me to sleep—or maybe that's the exhaustion. We spent hours last night in bed, exploring all the different ways two people can have sex in a remote mountain cabin.

Well, not *all* of them. I'm pretty sure we didn't even make a dent in the mountain man's Kama Sutra. But we tried.

Shivering as my nerves get the best of me, I tug the blankets up higher. West will be here in a couple of hours, and I don't want to leave Wyatt—and lose whatever this is between us. But he's right. Living in the middle of nowhere with only Wyatt and Murphy around? I can't do that either. I need people. Technology. Takeout. Central heat.

I drain the last of the coffee and trudge into the bathroom. I'm deliciously sore all over, yet I'd jump Wyatt again in a heartbeat. He woke me this morning with his massive erection pressed to my ass, and we passed an hour slowly. Tenderly.

I always thought the phrase "making love" was stupid. It's sex. Fucking. A roll in the sheets. Or it always has been.

Not with Wyatt though. Not today.

We most definitely made love.

After a quick shower, I pull on the new clothes from the General Store. The jeans and t-shirt both hang off of me. When I first met Simon, I was curvy. I loved how I looked. How I felt. But thanks to three years of the world's strictest diet, I'm now so thin, my hipbones stick out and I can see most of my ribs.

The socks fit, at least. And once I have my boots zipped, I make two cups of instant coffee and carry them outside to find Wyatt.

Crisp, spring air scented with pine greets me, and I'm shocked at the change since yesterday. Murphy barks in the distance, happy, like he's chasing squirrels—or whatever dogs chase in the middle of nowhere—and a gentle breeze ruffles my hair.

Wyatt's flannel shirt hangs on a tree branch. His t-shirt strains over his broad back, each swing of the axe coiling his muscles in a way that makes my core heat and my nipples tighten.

"Hey." I stop a few feet away, waiting until he sees me before I offer him the mug. "Thought you might want this."

The furrow between his brows that appeared not long after he made breakfast is deeper now, and his shoulders hike up around his ears. "I want you."

"You had me. Three times last night and once this morning." Smiling into my cup, I realize I actually *like* instant coffee. And what Wyatt does to my body.

"That's not what I meant." He drops the axe next to a tree stump the size of a small car, brushes splinters and bits of wood off the flat surface, and sinks down, resting his head in his hands.

"Then what—?"

Murphy races into the clearing—utterly silent—and skids to a stop in front of Wyatt, pawing the ground, then Wyatt's foot.

My mountain man is instantly on alert. Standing, he grabs the axe, then his flannel shirt. "Hope? You're going to the basement. Right fucking now. Lock the door from the inside and stay completely silent." He wraps strong fingers around my elbow and pulls me toward the cabin.

"What is it?" I hiss. My heart pounds so hard, I'm sure he can hear it. Murphy stays close. The dog's ears are perked up, and his head swivels from side to side.

"I'm going to find out." At the basement door, he leans in, his lips brushing my ear. "Stay put until you hear me say 'firefly.' Understand? No other word."

"Firefly?" I'm confused. And scared. I clutch his forearm. "Wyatt—"

"Firefly. If anything happens to me and West comes for you, he knows the code word too. Do *not* open the door without it." Wyatt hauls me against him. The kiss is so passionate that, for a moment, I forget how terrified I am. Until Murphy whines. With a nod, Wyatt deposits me on the second step. "Lock it. Now."

The door slams, and suddenly, everything makes sense. There's someone here. Someone who doesn't belong.

Simon's men. They've come for me.

I flip both locks. They're heavy. So is the door. And when it shut, it didn't sound like *just* wood. Duller somehow. God, I hope it's reinforced.

Shit. The memory card is still in the safe. They won't be able to get it, will they? Does it even matter? If they find me, I'll wish I were dead. They'll kill Wyatt. Murphy too. Tears burn my eyes. Sinking down onto the steps, I pray we'll find some way out of this. That I haven't signed the death warrant for the man I just might be falling for.

Wyatt

My dog—my best friend—paws at the floor. "I know, pal. Hold." I'm not going anywhere without my Glock, my rifle, and the memory card. No way in hell is that asshole getting a hold of it. I'll eat the damn thing if I have to.

At least Murph's ears aren't twitching yet. Whoever he saw —or heard—is at least half a mile away. Holster jammed onto my belt. Two extra mags in my pockets. The memory card gets tucked into the waistband of my briefs. Not the best place in the world, but a hell of a lot less obvious than in the safe.

On the way out the door, I snag the rifle and my small rucksack. "Target," I whisper to Murphy. "Quiet."

He bares his teeth, scenting the air, then darts left into the underbrush. We're a team. Before I took him on his first mission, we trained together for over a year. He knows what to do. How far ahead he can get. And how to warn me if someone's too close.

Not knowing how many of them are out there, I draw the pistol. The solid weight in my hand is familiar. Like an extension of my arm. Slinging the rifle over my shoulders, I scan the trees all around me for any unnatural movement.

It's almost noon. Sampson should be close. Fuck. What I wouldn't give for cell service right now.

Two thumps in the bushes straight ahead. Murphy's tail. He's locked onto a scent. When I reach him, I lower myself to one knee.

He's the most intelligent animal I've ever met, but he can't talk. Can't tell me how many there are or what weapons they have on them. I rest my hand on his collar, then point to the ground. He drops to his belly, a single low growl coming from his throat.

A flash of dark fabric moves fifty yards to the north.

"Hold," I whisper.

The Glock goes back in the holster, and I switch to the rifle. Better for long range. Through my sights, I get a closer look at the assholes. There are two of them, and if they didn't pose such a serious threat to Hope's safety, I'd laugh.

Black pants, black *sweaters*, and black boots. Not the hiking kind. Hell, they're polished so well, the sun glares off the leather.

I just need them to come a little closer. From this angle, I can't tell if they're armed. The chance they're civilians is less than point-oh-two percent of nothing, but I need some confirmation before I end them.

They're making so much noise, I don't know how these assholes expected to sneak up on anyone. *Amateurs.*

And then I hear a *snap* from behind me. Shit. Something hits my shoulder. The pop was so quiet, it had to be from a silenced weapon.

"Cover!" I grunt, and Murphy takes off like the devil himself is on his heels. A fiery pain starts to spread from the point of impact, and my fingers spasm. I can't hold onto the rifle, and it hits the ground. Fuck.

"Shoot the goddamn dog!" a harsh voice orders, and I collapse onto my right side, pulling the pistol from its holster as I do. There's no way these shitheads are going to kill my dog. Over my dead body.

Footsteps pound through the underbrush, closer by the second. No time to run. I can use this.

"Where is she?" One of those shiny boots presses to my shoulder. Pure agony rips through me. The man forces me onto my back. I should see the sky, but dark spots blot out the sun.

I don't aim. This close, I don't have to. The 9mm hollow point tears through the fuckwit's chest, and his eyes go wide and glassy.

Motion to my left has me pushing to my knees. "Come out now and I'll make it quick. Hurt my dog, and you're gonna find out what your own ball sack tastes like, assholes."

A shot hits the tree above me. Bits of bark slice my cheek, but I don't care. My right arm is mostly useless, but I can shoot well enough with my left. I have to draw these pigfuckers away from the cabin. And Hope.

Hope

Wyatt's basement is like a prepper's wet dream. Fully stocked with canned goods, gallon jugs of water, cleaning supplies, tools, fishing gear, and more. A clothesline stretches across the room with a pair of jeans and a flannel shirt draped over it.

My arm aches, and I rub my palms on my thighs. I hate not knowing what's going on. Hate being trapped in a dim, windowless room. Too many memories of all the times Simon punished me.

My heart races. I have to get out of here. But I can't leave. Not until Wyatt comes back for me. I promised.

What if they've already killed him?

Oh, God. No. Please, no.

If I don't do *something*, I'll scream. So I search through a large rolling tool cabinet until I find a hammer.

This is better. I can defend myself.

With a hammer, Hope? This is a joke, right?

The *crack* from outside makes me yelp, and the hammer hits the cement floor. Another loud bang, and I realize what I'm hearing.

Gunshots.

A scrambling, scratching sound comes from the far end of the room. There's nothing over there but shelves and storage boxes. Shit. I have to hide. I drop to my knees and try to wedge myself under the utility sink.

It's too small. Too tight. Too exposed.

Wyatt. Please come back.

Murphy yips, and then he's nosing my elbow. "How did you get in here?" I wrap my arms around his sleek body. Something sticks to my palm, and I pull back.

Blood.

My heart skips a beat. Or five. "Is Wyatt hurt?"

The dog whines, then tugs on the sleeve of my sweatshirt. That's a yes if I ever heard one.

"Show me the door," I say softly, crawling out from under the sink.

Murphy trots to the back corner, stops, and glances back at me before nosing the wall. A doggie door swings open, and a shaft of sunlight streams into the room.

"You want me to squeeze through that?" Eyeing the opening, I shove a cardboard box aside and crouch down. I could just go back up the stairs. But as soon as I push to my feet, footsteps cross the floor above me. More than one set.

That's not Wyatt. He doesn't make a sound when he walks. And Murphy's growing more agitated by the second. He keeps sticking his head back through the opening and whining.

"Go," I tell him, and he's through the door like a shot. Lying on the floor, I shove my arms outside first. The movement pulls at my stitches, and I stifle my whimper. Head. Shoulders. Chest. My boots scramble for purchase. Murphy dips his head and tries to nose under my right elbow. He's so damn smart. As soon as I wrap my arms around his neck, he starts pulling me.

My hips catch on the edge of the door. Shit. I force all the air from my lungs, desperate for just a fraction of an inch. Gritting my teeth, I kick once, and I'm free.

The soft earth is still damp from the snowmelt, but early spring wildflowers carpet the landscape. Murphy noses my cheek, whining softly, before he grabs the collar of my sweatshirt in his teeth and tugs once.

I get it. Time to get the hell away from here.

Resting my hand on the back of the dog's neck, I lean close and whisper, "Find Wyatt."

Murphy stares at me for a beat, and I swear there's a gleam in his eyes as he takes off. I follow as quietly as I can, but with every step, I cringe. I sound like a herd of elephants running through the woods.

Two loud bangs send me scurrying behind a large pine tree. A few seconds later, a handful of quieter pops come from a different direction.

I know that sound. One of Simon's generals tried to leave the organization once. Simon made me watch while Brix shot the man with a silenced pistol.

"Murphy. Wait." I don't dare raise my voice. If I weren't so worried about Wyatt, I'd find a tree and try to climb it. Not that I know how. "Where is he?" Those luminous eyes lock onto mine for a moment before he stares in the direction of the louder shots. "You better be right."

Murphy stays at my side, herding me in a roundabout fashion toward where I hope Wyatt is. I think he's protecting me. Making sure I don't run right into Simon's men. At least, I hope he is.

Another shot rings out. This one can't be more than fifty feet away.

Oh, God. I can see him. Sitting behind a tree, the rifle braced on his bent leg. His right arm hangs at his side, blood dripping from his fingers.

At Murphy's quick, low yip, Wyatt whips his head around. His eyes widen. "I told you to stay put," he growls.

"You're hurt." Kneeling next to him, I hold out my hand. "Give me the pistol. I can help."

Wyatt

What the fuck?

"You know how to shoot?"

Shards of tree bark pelt my arm as Tweedle Dee and Tweedle Dude Ranch Wannabe try to get a clean shot.

"Yes. And blame Murphy for me being here. *He's* the one who came to get me. Thank God, because I heard two guys upstairs as I was crawling out the doggie door."

My jaw drops open until another shot grazes my wounded arm. It's barely a scratch but comes way too close to Murph for my liking. "I *told* you," I shout and pull the Glock 19 from the holster, "if you hurt my dog, there's gonna be hell to pay!" One of the assholes is close enough I can probably get him with the handgun. "Cover your ears, darlin'."

She rolls her eyes, but does it. The agonized groan as my bullet finds its mark is satisfying as fuck.

"We have to get out of here. Head towards the highway. Sampson should be close." As much as I hate to ask, I don't have a choice. "You any good with a rifle? It's gonna be damn near impossible for me to hit anything with it on the move."

"Probably better than you are right now. But I never touched one outside of the gun range." Despite her words, she picks it up. "What about the memory card? We can't leave it."

"We didn't." Getting to my feet makes the pain in my shoulder flare white hot, and I lean on the tree for support until the world stops spinning. "You stick to me like glue."

"Promise." She's terrified. I can see it in her eyes. But this Hope? She's not the scared, timid little mouse I pulled out of that SUV. This is who she was meant to be. A fighter.

And I want the chance for a future with her.

"Murphy." The dog looks up at me, and I point in the general direction of the highway. "Exfil."

He takes off like someone just lit his ass on fire. We're going to need a fucking miracle to get out of here alive. Two of them at the cabin. At least two more—in addition to the one I killed —close by. How many others?

Murphy stops short and growls. A twig snaps, and a man steps out from behind a tree ten yards in front of us.

"Hold, Murph!" I draw down on the guy, but he's smiling. Six-feet two-inches of burly asshole in a thousand-dollar suit. Grinning at us.

At my side, Hope sucks in a sharp breath. "Brix..."

"You have been a very bad girl," Brix says. "Simon knows what you did."

Fuck this. I'm about to pull the trigger when two black-clad thugs flank us. One presses the barrel of a Sig Sauer to my forehead, and the other aims at Murphy.

"If I were you," Brix waves his hand in my general direction, "I would toss the pistol behind you. Before Matteo gets twitchy."

I don't have a choice. Not if I want to live more than another few seconds. The gun lands on the mossy ground with a dull thud, and now that my left hand is free, I link my fingers with Hope's. "Happy now, shitstain?"

"Hardly. I won't be happy until I return to *civilization*. With Ms. Raines in tow. Or rather, tied up in the trunk of the car. Simon wants her to have a very painful ride back to Salt Lake City." He arches his brows. "Come quietly, and maybe I won't shoot the dog."

"Touch him, and I'll—"

Asshole Number Two slams the gun against the back of my head. Stars explode in my field of vision, and my knees buckle.

"Wyatt!" Hope grabs me. I groan as the agony in my shoulder turns the whole world bright white. My heartbeat roars in my ears, but her voice pierces the din. "Let him live—Murphy too—and I'll go with you."

What? Oh, hell no.

Shaking off the haze of pain, I straighten. "Hope, you are not going with this pile of shit."

"I have to." Tears line her eyes, and she touches my cheek. The rifle still hangs from her shoulder. She's no threat to Brix or any of his men. He knows it. Not with the two on either side of us ready to shoot me for breathing too loudly. "I can't let him hurt you too." Without taking her eyes off me, she says, "Wyatt isn't a threat to anyone, Brix. He's just a guy who wanted to spend the rest of his life in the middle of nowhere. He doesn't have a phone or a car or even a computer."

When she turns to him, the dickwad is grinning. "We're leaving. Now." He snaps his fingers. "Come. Here."

Hope leans in and brushes her lips to mine.

No. I will *not* let her go like this. This woman is it for me. I can't lose her. I don't care what I have to do. Live in a big city? Done. Move to a *war zone?* I wouldn't give it a second thought.

There is no fucking way that sadistic idiot in Salt Lake City is ever laying a hand on her—chirping. The sound comes from my ten o'clock. That's not a bird. Sliding my hand up to tangle in Hope's dark locks, I kiss her for all I'm worth, until I hear five more high-pitched notes.

Brix turns beet red. When I let Hope come up for air, a vein in his forehead starts to throb.

Four chirps.

"Don't do this, Hope." I wish I had a way to tell her what's coming. All I can do now is stall. "Murphy needs you. *I* need you." Reaching down to stroke the dog's ears, I tap his neck and rest my fingers on the top of his head.

Three.

"We could have a future," I say quietly.

"Not if they kill you." Her tears fall, and she stares down at her feet. "I put you in danger. This is the only way they'll let you and Murphy live. Trust me, Wyatt. Hold on to the memories we made."

Two.

The memory card. She really does think I'm going to let her go.

"Darlin'? You remember what I said to you the first night? About how I'd always be honest with you? About why I didn't lie?"

Her gaze softens, and she swipes at her cheek. "I'll never forget."

One.

"Something else you should know about men like me." In one fluid movement, I grab her around the waist and take her to the ground. Three quick shots, followed by three bodies hitting the soft spring grass. "We have friends."

Murphy sprints through the trees, and five seconds later, the last of the men screams. I roll with Hope until we reach the pistol, and when the coward stumbles into view, I put a bullet through his heart.

"Sampson!" I call as Murphy bounds up to us, drops onto his haunches, and stares at me with a self-satisfied expression in his eyes. "About fucking time."

12

Wyatt

"You're welcome." West Sampson drops out of a tree fifty yards to the north. Dressed in a pair of black pants and a dark blue Henley, he slings his M4 over his shoulder. "Damn lucky I spotted the last one when I pulled off the road. He was operating a drone, giving the other dumbfucks directions. Would have been here sooner, but I had to neutralize him and his goddamn machine."

Hope shudders underneath me. I get to my feet, help her up, and tuck her against my side. "You okay, darlin'?"

"Wh-what just happened?" Her dazed expression worries me, but at least she's not freaking the fuck out.

"West happened." Heading for the man who just saved our lives—and ended four others—I try not to let Hope see just how much pain I'm in. "Hope, this is West Sampson. Retired Navy SEAL and a damn good shot."

"Hi...?" As if she's just realized Brix and his men are dead only ten feet away, her knees buckle, and I tighten my hold on her. "Sorry. I'm...um...dizzy."

"Adrenaline crash. Lean on me." I whistle for Murphy, and he bounds over to us, his tongue hanging out of his mouth like he's just found the biggest stash of kibble in the world. "Can we take this inside?" I ask.

"You go. I need to confirm the kills first. Don't suppose you have a tarp?" He's tense—he will be until he knows without a doubt none of the men are getting back up again. And that there aren't any more of them.

"In the shed." I point to the small outbuilding at the edge of the clearing, then guide Hope back to the cabin. Blood still drips from my fingers, and if I don't sit down soon, I'll fall down. But I don't give a shit how much it hurts. We're safe—for now—and that's all that matters.

That and telling Hope that I don't want to let her go. I'll do whatever it takes to make this work. If she'll have me.

"They found us," she murmurs—almost to herself. "You said..."

"Wren can control satellite scans. Not some stupid motherfucker with a drone. I can't believe I didn't hear it. Must have been a damn good one."

I sink onto the couch, grunting as the movement pulls at the fresh bullet wound. The sound snaps Hope out of her daze, and she sucks in a sharp breath. "Where's your first aid kit?"

"Leave it, darlin'. I'll be fine. I'd rather just hold you right now."

"Bullshit," she mutters. "You're bleeding all over the place."

I peer down at my arm and snort. "This is nothing. Been through worse. Come here."

Hope wraps her arms around my waist and nestles her cheek against my neck. I'm tired. Tired and sore and mad as hell. Those fuckers were in my cabin. They threatened my dog—and the woman I'm falling in love with.

Holy shit.

The realization hits me so hard, it steals my breath. I don't just care for this woman. I'm falling for her. Hard and fast and forever. Why didn't I see it before? I knew I didn't want to let her go. But love? I can't *love* her. Can I?

"Wyatt? Oh, God. Are you still with me?" Hope frames my face with her hands, and I blink hard until I can focus. "You need a doctor."

"I need *you*. Hope, I thought I could let you go—"

The back door closes with a *bang*. West trudges over to the kitchen sink and turns the faucet on full blast. "You're lucky I had the M4 in the truck," he says as he starts scrubbing his hands. "My Glock wouldn't have done shit from that far away."

"Lucky? You're like a fucking Boy Scout, West. Always prepared for anything."

He chuckles, but sobers almost immediately once he glances over at me. "Just *had* to get yourself shot, didn't you? Towels in the bathroom? I'll stitch you up."

Hope's eyes widen. "He needs a hospital."

"West is a field medic, darlin'. And hospitals ask too many questions. I'll be fine. If the bullet had hit an artery, I'd be dead already." It's the wrong thing to say by a thousand miles, and I'd kick myself if I had the energy. Instead, I squeeze her tighter and pray I'll find the strength to tell her how I feel.

Twenty minutes—and a shot of bourbon—later, I pull on a clean shirt, careful not to tear the fresh stitches in my shoulder. Hope is tucked under a blanket on the couch with Murphy lying across her lap.

"Mind if I borrow your ATV?" West asks, leaning against the bedroom door jamb. "My truck won't handle this terrain, and I'm sure as shit not lugging those bodies up to the road one at a time."

"Keys are on the peg by the door." My duffel bag lands on the bed, and West arches his brows. "Don't," I warn. "Don't say a goddamn word. She still thinks she's leaving without me."

Ambling over to my dresser, West picks up the framed photo of our Trident ceremony. "We're the only two left."

"No shit." I regret my words almost immediately. Eight men in the picture, and three of them died when West and his team were ambushed outside of Kabul years ago. "Sorry. I'm an ass."

With a shrug, West passes me the frame. "Living alone will do that to you."

"I was an ass before I moved up here. You know that." Dumping a bunch of socks and briefs into the duffel bag, I head for my closet. We're not staying here a minute longer than we have to. Thank fuck I don't need more than a few pairs of jeans and half a dozen flannel shirts. "Get the bodies to your truck. I'll talk to Hope. And warn Ryker, will you? Because if he gives me shit for coming back to the city, I won't be responsible for my actions."

West chuckles. "Good luck with that, man. You punch Ry, he's gonna knock you into next week. But don't worry. We'll keep Hope safe until you regain consciousness."

"Fucker," I say under my breath. "Go. I want to be on our way to Seattle within the hour."

Hope

The jangling of keys draws my gaze from the waning fire in the woodstove. West hoists his pack on one shoulder, and I sit up straighter. "You're leaving?"

"Not yet. Just gotta load the bodies into my truck. I'll be back in half an hour. Maybe less." West's slight accent—something southern—is oddly reassuring, except that he's talking about five dead men like they're a load of topsoil.

"You're...taking them?" I don't know why I'm surprised. Except I thought the police would be involved. Until I realize that West and Wyatt would probably be arrested for murder. And I'd be to blame. "I'm sorry, I just..."

I can *feel* the blood draining from my cheeks, and West drops his pack. Before I know what's happening, he's holding my hand and rubbing slow circles on the inside of my wrist. "Count to ten, Hope. Focus on my voice and count with me. One..."

I can't. Murphy whines and presses his nose to my neck. I'd hold him. If I could move.

"Wyatt! Get out here," West calls. He drops my hand and, seconds later, Wyatt pulls me against him.

"I've got you, darlin'. Breathe." His deep voice rumbles through me, his scent calming me in a way nothing else can. It takes several moments, but the darkness threatening my vision fades. My heart no longer feels like it's about to explode. If only I could stop shaking.

"I'm okay," I manage.

"You're not. Don't lie to me." Coming from anyone else, those words would terrify me. But from Wyatt, they're reassuring. He'll protect me until his last breath. As long as we're together, anyway. "Look at me. Please?"

With a shuddering sigh, I draw back to meet his gaze. "When Brix doesn't check in, Simon will send another team. A bigger one. You can't fight them alone—"

He cracks a weary smile. "Not planning on it. West's team will take care of everything. This is what they do."

"I thought you said there were only five of them?" I don't understand how he's so calm. Or how I'm supposed to leave him in an hour. I'll never see him again. "Simon has dozens of guys. Hell, he probably has hundreds! You're all alone up here."

"Not staying up here. I'm going to Seattle with you."

He says it so matter-of-factly, I think he has to be joking. But there's no humor in his eyes. "Wyatt, you hate the city." I can't begin to explain how much I want him to come, but there's no way I'll ask him to leave the one place he feels at home.

"Not as much as I care—fuck it—not as much as I think I could love you, Hope."

Shock steals my next words. "You think...?"

The kiss is hard and fast and everything I've ever wanted. Possessive, yet tender. Passionate, but almost gentle by the end. And when our lips part, he cups my cheek, his thumb skating lightly over my skin. "It's too soon. I know it is. I don't care. I don't want to lose you," he says, his voice rough. "But you have to tell me what *you* want. If you're not okay with me going with you, I'll find a place in Seattle on my own. I'll get a cell phone so you can contact me. In case you ever decide—"

I throw my arms around him, then quickly adjust when I catch his shoulder and he grunts. "I don't want to go anywhere without you. Whatever happens next, I need you with me. The rest we'll figure out as we go."

Wyatt

Murphy snores from the second row of seats in West's truck. Hope is tucked in the crook of my arm. She fell asleep not more than ten minutes after the two-mile hike from my cabin to the highway. I hate leaving the place—especially since this Simon fuckwad knows where I live. But it's the only way to keep her safe, and that's all that matters to me.

"Coffee?" West asks when I stifle my yawn. He gestures to a couple of thermoses in the center console. "Help yourself."

"You're a life saver." After a long swig, I stifle a moan. "Holy fuck. Instant coffee is shit compared to this."

He laughs, then slaps his hand over his mouth and glances at Hope.

"She's not a light sleeper," I say quietly. "At least, I don't think so."

With a quick check of the mirrors, West merges onto Interstate 90. "Exactly how long have you known this woman, anyway?"

"Forty-one hours." At his arched brows, I tighten my arm around her. "Don't look at me like that. When you know, you know."

The man chokes down a swig of coffee. "When you know, you know? Are you telling me you're *in love* with her after forty-one hours?"

"Maybe. Haven't figured that part out yet. I think I could be heading there."

"Damn."

Hope shifts against me, and her eyelids flutter open. "What's going on?"

"Nothing, darlin'. You fell asleep. We still have another two hours before we get to Seattle." I press a kiss to her temple and hope she'll rest more, but instead, she sits up, her gaze zeroing in on the thermos.

"Is that coffee?"

With a chuckle, West nods. "Help yourself. It's not instant, though. Hope you like it strong."

"I used to live on quad-shot Americanos," she says, her lips quirking into a smile. She hums a little as she takes a sip. "Oh, God. This is amazing. Wyatt, I'm sorry. Your coffee doesn't hold a candle to this."

I roll my eyes. "West is a coffee snob."

"Watch your language. Or Hope and I will drink the rest and you'll be left with nothing." He winks, and Hope clutches the thermos to her chest. "Plus, I seem to remember you were too the last time you lived in Seattle."

"Maybe." I shrug, aggravating my shoulder. I'm about to turn my focus out the window when Hope passes me the insulated container.

"I'll share," she says. "I'm not used to the caffeine hit anymore. Too much and I'll start vibrating."

"Not used to—?" West frowns. "You *gave up* coffee?"

With that single question, Hope's entire demeanor changes. She shrinks against me, dropping her gaze to the floor and clenching her jaw so hard, I can hear her teeth grind together.

"West, don't," I warn.

"It's okay. He's going to find out the whole story eventually." She sighs, but still refuses to look anywhere but the floor mat. "Simon didn't drink coffee. Or anything with caffeine. No meat, no dairy. No junk food. I haven't had a candy bar or soda or a hamburger in more than three years."

"Holy shit. Not even when you went out?" West asks.

Fuck me. Why didn't I tell West what she'd been through earlier? The pain etched on her face shatters my heart into a million pieces, and when she sniffles and swipes at her nose, it's like all the tiny fragments catch fire.

"He never let me go out. I didn't—I don't—have a phone or clothes or money. I left with nothing..."

"Shhh, darlin'. It's all right." Holding her close, I glare at West over the top of her head. "That asshole doesn't get to control any part of your life ever again. No one's gonna tell you what to eat, what to wear, or what to say. Not while I'm around."

From the driver's seat, West clears his throat. "I'm sorry, Hope. I shouldn't have said anything."

"You didn't know," she says, her voice flat. "It's okay."

"It's not." Running a hand through his hair, the man blows out a breath. "How much did Wyatt tell you about me? About the group I work with?"

Hope sits up a little straighter, her gaze fixed out the side window. "Just that you were all badasses."

He laughs, checks the mirrors, and flips down the visor as we round a bend and sunlight glares through the windshield. "Well, he got that right. But a lot's changed since Wyatt last set foot in the city—any city."

"Fuck. Like what?" I ask.

"Everything? Ryker and Wren are married now. Though I think you knew that. Graham—he came to Hidden Agenda a couple of years ago—hooked up with his guy, Quinton, and we hired two more folks. Raelynn's been on a handful of ops already, and Caleb just started training."

"Is that all?" As relieved as I am that West, Inara, and Ryker have help, I don't know Graham, Quinton, Raelynn, or Caleb. How the fuck am I supposed to trust them?

"Shit. No. Ripper."

The coffee threatens to come out my nose. "Ripper? As in Sergeant Richards? He's dead."

West glances over at me, a haunted look in his eyes. "Not anymore."

NINETY MINUTES LATER, the coffee's gone, and the Seattle city limits sign comes into view.

"Let me get this straight," I say. "The jackhole who tortured Ripper for six fucking years just happened to kidnap the long lost love of Dax's business partner?"

"Yup." West shakes his head. "Pretty damn stupid of him. But he's dead now."

"You know this shit only happens in books, right?"

West shoots me an amused look. "If everything we do wasn't completely illegal, I'd say it'd make a good story."

Hope's right leg bounces against my thigh. She's vibrating

with nerves—and caffeine. I'm not doing much better. I haven't been around people in so long, I don't know how to act. Or how to control the anxiety twisting itself into a knot in my chest.

West assures us we'll be safe. That Ryker McCabe bought a whole goddamn building not far from downtown and outfitted every unit with bulletproof privacy glass, top-of-the-line security systems, and encrypted hardline internet.

He tucks a small, black comms unit into his ear and taps it twice. "Ry? We're twenty minutes out." After a pause, he adds, "Yup. Have Wren send it to my phone. "

Another two taps, and he glances over at me. "We're going right from the secured parking garage to the elevator. Wren's monitoring the security cameras, so there shouldn't be any surprises, but keep Hope between us. You're in unit 507. Ripper and Cara have 501, with Graham and Q in 511. Ry and Wren took over the whole top floor. The only other occupied units in the building are folks we've worked with before. They're vetted to hell and back, so you'll be safe."

"Simon has people everywhere..." Hope says quietly. "You're *sure?*"

West offers her a weary smile. "Wren's seven months pregnant. If Ry could, he'd bubble wrap the whole world for her. When they found out about the baby, he had her run every single background check a second time. And a third. Then had Zephyr—she works in Boston with another group we sometimes partner with—double check her work. That...didn't go over so well with Wren. Pretty sure Ry slept on the floor for a few nights."

The idea of that tiny, petite redhead putting Ryker McCabe in his place is so amusing, I have to stifle my chuckle when West continues. "And then he upgraded the elevator access. The other tenants can't access anything above the fourth floor."

Hope relaxes slightly, but she's still wound so tight, she could break at any moment.

"Ryker doesn't take chances, darlin'," I say when I drape my arm around her shoulders. "Once you meet him, you'll understand. He's...intense."

West barks out a laugh and merges on to Interstate 5. "That's the understatement of the year."

13

Hope

SANDWICHED between Wyatt and West with Murphy padding along behind us, I try not to panic at being somewhere vaguely public—even though West had to punch in a long string of numbers on the garage security panel, scan his thumbprint, *and* say some sort of passphrase before the gate opened.

"Ry and Wren will set you up with your own access codes, voice prints, and phones," West says when we're in the elevator. "Anything you need—clothes, food, supplies—we'll get for you."

Anything?

In my world—the world I've lived in for the past three years —no one offered me a single thing that didn't come with a steep price. If I had a choice, I wouldn't take anything from West and his team. But I have nothing.

No. You have Wyatt. For now, at least.

I don't know what I expected. That I'd show up in Seattle, hand over the memory card, and just...start a new life? Walk down the street without fear? Go to a coffee shop and people watch? Have dinner in a restaurant and order whatever I wanted?

I can't do any of those things.

The elevator doors whisper open to a long, well-lit hallway. "No blind corners." West points to small, beige boxes spaced at regular intervals along the ceiling. "Security cameras monitor 24x7, and all the footage feeds into Wren's facial recognition programs. Anyone trips her system, and alarms go off. Ry, Graham, and Ripper will be at your door in minutes. Probably less."

Wyatt keeps his arm around me as West stops in front of Unit 507 and enters another long series of numbers on the keypad next to the door.

"Oh, my God." My breath catches in my throat. The apartment is gorgeous. Huge floor-to-ceiling windows, French doors that lead out onto a balcony, plush carpeting. Muted blue walls, fluffy couches. A vase overflowing with flowers on the kitchen counter. It's welcoming and oh so peaceful. Different in every way from the perfect, museum-like atmosphere of Simon's compound.

West hovers in the doorway. "There are two bedrooms down the hall, and the fridge should be stocked with some basics. Take a few minutes to settle in. I'm going upstairs to give Ry a quick debrief before I take care of the load of shit in my truck," he says, his hand on the doorknob. "Wyatt, if you need to take Murphy out before Ry comes down, press 701 on the security panel and it'll connect you to him. He'll handle the building access."

Wyatt nods, but doesn't say a word. When West leaves, I turn to him, my hands on his hips. "You hate this. Don't you?"

He doesn't meet my gaze. Just stares out the windows at the setting sun. "It's quiet up here. Where I lived before..." With a shrug and a wince, he pulls away and adjusts his duffel bag on his shoulder. "There were sirens all the time. Traffic noise too.

Not the best area of town. Come on, Murph. Let's get your bed set up."

Man and dog amble down the hall, looking completely out of their element in the luxurious, almost feminine space. I wander over to the French doors and press my palms to the glass. Am I allowed to go outside? Not knowing amps the anxiety churning in my belly, so I retreat and sink onto the overstuffed light blue sofa and tuck my legs under me.

Maybe letting Wyatt come with me was a mistake.

But if he stayed up in the mountains, Simon would find him.

He's safe here. Even if he is miserable.

Murphy bounds down the hall with a rawhide bone in his mouth, looking like he just found the Holy Grail. The pure joy in his eyes makes me smile. "Whatcha got there, buddy?" He's so smart—or so eager to share his treasure—that he drops the very wet, very slimy bone in my lap.

Ew. I shouldn't have asked.

"Murph." Wyatt snaps his fingers, and the dog picks up the bone, then settles at my feet. "Sorry. He loves those damn things."

I'm about to tell him it's okay when a chime sounds. Murphy drops his prize, bolts to the door, and bares his teeth.

"Go into the bedroom," Wyatt snaps. "Now."

My heart hammers against my ribs. No one knows we're here. They can't.

"Hope..."

The doorbell—what else can it be?—sounds again, seconds before there's an electronic click from a speaker, then a man's rough voice. "Wyatt, open the goddamn door."

"Murph. Friend." The dog returns to his bone, and Wyatt holds out his hand for me. "It's Ryker. Come here, darlin'."

Tucking me under his arm, he flips the sturdy locks and steps back as the door swings inward. Oh, my God. I thought Wyatt was huge, but the man in the hall is a giant. Scars cover half his bald head and the left side of his face then wind down his neck before disappearing under a tight, black t-shirt. He's obviously ripped, and I'm pretty sure he could bench-press a car.

The woman at his side doesn't even reach his shoulder. Her billowy green sweatshirt matches her eyes, and red, wavy locks tumble around her heart-shaped face.

"About damn time," Ryker says. His lips twitch into what might almost be a smile. "Never thought I'd see you back in Seattle, Wyatt."

"Ry."

The men stare one another down for so long, the redhead rolls her eyes. "Will the two of you get over yourselves? My feet are permanently swollen these days and I have to pee. *Again*." She turns her focus to me. "I'm Wren. You must be Hope. Can I use your bathroom?"

"Um, hi. And...sure?"

Wren thrusts a messenger bag into my hands. "Thanks. Be right back!" She's down the hall before I know what to say. Or how to react to the tension between the two alpha men in front of me.

"You gonna invite me in?" Ryker asks. "Or are we doing this standing in the doorway?"

Wyatt takes a step back with me and shrugs his uninjured shoulder. "It's your place, Ry. We're just borrowing it for a spell."

"For fuck's sake." Ryker moves with a grace a man his size shouldn't possess. I expect to feel the floor vibrate with his every step, but he's utterly silent as he crosses to the French doors. For a beat, I can only see his broad back as he stares out over the city skyline. Then his shoulders heave and he turns to face us again. "You saved my life, Wyatt. We're...family."

The last word seems to stick in Ryker's throat, and from the look on Wyatt's face, it wasn't what he expected to hear. He gapes at the big man until Ryker rolls his eyes. They're this odd mix of hazel, green, and blue, and the colors seem to shift as he fixes his stare on me.

"So you're Hope."

The urge to shrink behind Wyatt hits hard until Wren comes back down the hall. "Ry, you're doing that thing again."

"What thing?" I ask.

As intimidating as Ryker is, Wren's his complete opposite. She wraps her arm around Ryker's waist and melts into him. The man's entire demeanor changes when he peers down at her. His gaze softens, the tiny lines around his lips relax, and his eyes turn a deeper shade of...well...everything.

"Oh, you know," Wren says with a wave of her hand. "Big, terrifying, black ops soldier ready to burn down the world? Don't get me wrong. He could. He's done it a few times. But he's working on his inner teddy bear."

"H-his...wh-what?"

Don't laugh, Hope. Don't...

It's no use. Between the exasperation on Ryker's face and Wren's smile, I can't help myself.

"His inner teddy bear." She pats her swollen belly. "In just over two months, he's going to be singing lullabies and changing diapers. In between all the death and destruction. This one is going to turn him into a puddle of mush."

"For fuck's sake, little bird." Despite his words, Ryker's expression is pure love and adoration, and he leans down to press a kiss to the top of her head. "I am not—nor will I ever be —a 'puddle of mush.'"

Wren's laugh breaks the tension in the room, and for the first time since we arrived in Seattle, I feel something close to *normal*. "Of course not, soldier. You're a big, bad, growly fudger with a chip on your shoulder the size of the Space Needle." Lowering her voice, she winks at me. "And a puddle of mush."

"You should sit down," Ry says and guides Wren over to the

love seat. Wyatt and I take the couch, with Murphy at our feet. "You're not supposed to be on your feet for long."

"Oh, please. I've been on the couch all day. It took less than five minutes to get down here. The baby's *fine*, Ry. And so am I." Wren gestures to the messenger bag I'm still clutching to my chest. "Open it up. We brought presents."

Inside, I find two brand new smartphones, two tablets, and two wads of cash banded around multiple credit cards. "What...? This is too much," I protest.

Ryker snorts. "Standard relo pack. Tomorrow, we'll take some photos and get you new IDs. Both of you. The names on those cards both have good credit scores, employment histories, and tax records. Memorize them and use them whenever you talk to anyone not on my team."

My heart sinks. Will I ever be Hope Raines again?

"What's wrong, darlin'?" Wyatt takes my hand and squeezes gently.

"I just...this is a lot. I thought maybe...once I got away from Simon, that I'd be able to be...*me*." Tears prick my eyes, and I blink them away. "I was so stupid."

"You will be exactly who you want to be," Ryker growls, his voice so rough and commanding, I almost flinch. But like Wyatt, I get the sense that when Ryker gets angry, he keeps such a tight control on his emotions, he'd never hurt an innocent person. "This is what we do, Hope. It's what we've done for years, and we're really fucking good at it."

"He is—they are." Wyatt shifts to drape his arm around my shoulders. The heat of him helps center me. "Best in the world. Or at least the most stubborn."

"So," Ry says, settling back against the cushions while Wren opens her laptop and balances it on her knees. "Tell us everything we need to know."

Wyatt

Hope is curled on the couch with Murphy when the intercom chirps. “Meal Dash, Mr. Rourke. I’ll have the bag here for you at the security desk,” the friendly male voice says. Roarke. Wyatt Roarke. That’s who I am for the next...however long. The name feels wrong, but if that’s what it takes to keep Hope safe, I’ll keep it for the rest of my life.

I glance over at Hope to find fear in her eyes. “I’ll be gone five minutes, darlin’. The apartment’s secure. You have the panic button?”

She holds up her new cell phone. On the back of the case is the smallest transmitter I’ve ever seen. A triple tap alerts Ryker, Ripper, and Graham that she’s in trouble, and they all have the code to this place. We spent hours going over the various security protocols with Ry and Wren this evening—until Wren started yawning and Ryker insisted they go back to their top-floor unit so she could lie down.

We’ve gone through access codes, pass phrases, who we could and couldn’t call, text, or email—everyone outside of Ryker’s team is off limits—exfil procedures, even which takeout places have been vetted. More than once, Hope looked so overwhelmed, I insisted we take a break. But every time, she shook her head and said she wanted to keep going.

But now, she’s utterly silent. Come to think of it, she hasn’t uttered a single word since Ry and Wren left.

“I need to hear it, Hope. Will you be okay for five minutes?” I know she’s overwhelmed, but this is bordering on dissociation. I should know. I’m a pro at it.

Blinking hard, she focuses on me. “I’ll be fine. Go.”

There’s no emotion to her words, but at least it’s an answer. “Be right back. I think there are some beers in the fridge. Lemonade and pop too. Wine’s in the cabinet. I’ll have whatever you’re having.”

I wait until she gets up before I leave—the way she's acting I wouldn't be surprised if she stared off into space all night long. The large pizza, meatball sub, and two slices of cheesecake are waiting at the security desk in a secured lock box, and the guard makes me verify my new alias and the codeword before he'll give me the combination.

An ambulance speeds by outside the glass doors, its siren blaring loud enough, I break out in a cold sweat. The takeout containers hit the counter, and I back into the corner.

"Mr. Roarke? Are you all right?" the guard asks.

Hell no, I'm not all right. I'm about to come out of my skin. The flashing lights bore into my brain. They're all I can see. Until they fade away and my ass is on the floor. "Fuck."

"Wyatt?" The man's voice isn't familiar, and I peer up into a face easily ten years younger than my own. His blue eyes hold understanding, and he offers me his hand. "I'm Graham. That pizza yours? Smells damn good."

I let him help me to my feet. Shame burns my cheeks, but Graham just nudges the boxes toward me. "Better take those upstairs while they're still hot. Big Mario's is the best in town."

"Ry told you—"

Graham nods toward the elevator. Once the doors close, he leans against the far wall, and I finally notice the bag of gourmet cat food balanced on his hip. "We're all up to speed. The security guard's on Ry's payroll, but we still try not to say anything sensitive in front of him. We'll talk more tomorrow. Tonight, you and Hope should relax. Besides," he says with a wink, "I've got a home cooked meal waiting for me upstairs. And a very hungry kitten who's pissed we ran out of her favorite kibble."

I don't know what to say. Small talk isn't my thing. "Kitten?"

"Yeah. Clementine's a year old and climbing the walls. Literally. Found her at the top of the drapes this morning."

Before I can decide if I should laugh, we're back on the fifth floor. Graham pauses before we go our separate ways. "You need anything, we're right down the hall."

"Thanks," I say when he's halfway to his door. "For earlier. Sirens..."

"You don't need to explain. We've all been there."

I FIND Hope at the breakfast counter with plates and two glasses of wine set out for us. The scent of the food seems to perk her up, and she puts away three slices of salami primo and a piece of cheesecake. In almost complete silence.

If only she'd talk to me.

Idiot. You're not talking to her either.

What the fuck am I supposed to say? That one of Ry's men had to *rescue me* from the lobby because of a stupid siren? That I hate putting Murphy on a leash to take him out for a walk even though he couldn't care less?

Seattle hasn't been my home in more than three years. Yet sitting in this luxury apartment with Hope, I feel equal parts unsettled and more at peace than I have since I left the SEALs.

"You want to watch TV, darlin'?" I ask when the food's put away and the dishes are done. "Maybe a movie?"

Hope chews on her lip, her fingers stroking absently over Murphy's head. "I guess?"

Sinking down next to her, I cup the back of her neck and wait for her to meet my gaze. "What's wrong?"

"I don't know what I want, Wyatt. What I like. It's been so long since I could make *any* decisions for myself."

Her eyes shimmer with tears. Dammit. I want to find this Simon bastard and peel the flesh from his bones an inch at a time. Tomorrow, when Ry gets his team together, I'm going to insist he let me be the one to put an end to Arrens.

"Darlin', you can make *all* the decisions now. Here." I pass her the remote. "See what's on. If you watch five minutes of it and hate it, find something else."

"But...what if you—"

"No." Leaning closer, I brush my lips to hers. "You don't worry about what *I* want."

From the look on her face, she's about to protest—again—but I shake my head. "I want you to relax. To enjoy something—anything—as much as you savored that bacon the other day. Or the pizza tonight."

With a nod, Hope flips on the television. It's a full ten minutes before she settles on a station—some superhero movie from a couple of years ago—but when she leans against me and winds her arms around my waist, a lump swells in my throat. I'm falling in love with this woman. Anything she wants, anything she needs...I'll give her.

14

Wyatt

I'M up at first light, the soft-as-fuck sheets and duvet rustling as I ease Hope from my arms. Her sobs pulled me from a deep sleep sometime after midnight, but when I asked her to talk to me, she shook her head and claimed it was only a bad dream.

At least she let me hold her.

I didn't fare much better. Even got up at 3:00 a.m. to go sit out on the balcony with Murphy. This part of the city's quiet at night. Or maybe that's the five stories between us and the street. I could barely hear the sirens.

Murph follows me out to the kitchen and sits patiently as I start a pot of coffee—the good stuff, thanks to West—and dump a couple of scoops of food into his bowl. But he ignores it and pads over to the front door.

Fuck. Poor guy isn't used to being trapped indoors. "Five minutes, pal. Can't let Hope think we disappeared on her. Get your leash."

As soon as the coffee's done, I fill two travel mugs—one for me and one to leave on the nightstand for Hope—and scribble a quick note on the back of the takeout receipt from last night.

Taking Murphy out for a walk. Back soon. Call me if you need anything.

Call. On this hunk of plastic and glass I didn't ask for, but now don't want to be without. I shove the phone into my back pocket and pat my belt.

Shit. I locked my pistol in the safe built into the bedroom closet, and it needs to stay there. Without a concealed carry permit, I can't just walk down the street armed.

"You ready?" I ask, taking the leash from between Murphy's jaws and clipping it to his collar. He's so happy, his ass is wiggling. Either that or he *really* needs to take a piss.

Gotta hand it to Ryker and Wren. No one's getting past all these goddamn security protocols. I have to lock the front door with my palm print, and when Murph's done, it'll take a keycard, spoken passphrase, *and* a ten digit code to get back in.

The sun warms my back while Murphy waters the first tree he finds. Not many people out this early—thank God—and I start to relax.

Maybe this won't be as terrible as I'd feared.

The ground shakes as something big barrels my way from behind. The travel mug hits the concrete. I scan the sidewalk. Run. Hide. But there's nowhere to go.

A massive yellow and blue city bus rushes past us. Exhaust burns my nose. Along with the scent of coffee.

Murphy's front paws land on my chest and his cold tongue swipes at my cheek.

Get it together. It's a fucking bus. Not a Humvee. Or a tank. Or an RPG.

Yeah, tell that to my cross-wired brain. I'm shaking.

Stroking a hand down Murphy's back, I focus on his eyes. My best friend. The noise didn't bother him one bit. But he knew I needed him.

"Sorry, pal. Think there's any coffee left?" My voice cracks, and after I blow out a shaky breath, I wrap the end of his leash around my hand and retrieve the partial mug of coffee.

At least it's not all gone.

"Don't tell West," I mutter. "Or Hope. She doesn't need to worry about me."

Murphy trots along next to me, and we start doing circuits of the block so he can do his business and work off some of his pent-up energy. He's going to go batshit trapped inside all day. There has to be a dog park around here somewhere. A place he can run.

Hope's going to wake up soon, and I don't want her to be alone. Not for long. The apartment might be locked up tight, but that's part of the problem. She was a prisoner for three years. There's no way in hell I'm gonna let her feel like one now.

After breakfast—and a check-in with Ryker—maybe I'll take her shopping. Even though going out in public is the last thing I want to do.

Hope

Clutching Wyatt's note—and my new phone—to my chest, I open the French doors and step out onto the balcony. A gentle breeze ruffles my long hair.

"Tomorrow, we'll take some photos and get you new IDs."

I need scissors. Going to a stylist is so far out of the realm of possibility, I won't even ask, but I have to do *something* to feel more like *me* again.

In front of the bathroom mirror, I part my hair into sections and pick up the kitchen shears. Can I really do this?

Simon locked up everything sharper than a ball point pen,

and for three years, he refused to let me touch my hair. *"It looks better long, my sweet."*

Yeah, right. He just wanted it long so he could grab it to control me. I lost count of the number of times he dragged me by my long locks to that tiny room in the center of the compound. Once, I was so desperate, I tried to saw through the strands with a nail file. He found me. Then started bringing in a manicurist every two weeks. One he paid very well not to listen to anything I had to say.

The first strands cascade into the sink. It's so liberating, my eyes burn. Following the line of my jaw, I keep cutting. The back probably looks like shit, but all I can see in the mirror is a short, angled bob, longer in front, that frames my face and makes me look like a completely different person.

Or maybe that's just how I feel.

My phone vibrates on the counter, and the scissors clatter to the floor. Shit.

Wyatt: Coming back up with Murph.

My hands shake, panic sitting like a lead weight in my stomach. The bathroom's a mess. Why did I think this was a good idea?

The door locks *thunk* from the other room, and drop to my knees, frantically trying to push the errant strands of hair littering the tile floor into a pile.

"Hope?" Wyatt calls.

Don't come in. Don't come in. Don't come in.

"Um, give me a minute!"

It's too late. He towers over me from the doorway. My heart leaps into my throat. "I...I'm cleaning it up. Just need—"

"Stop, darlin'." He crouches down next to me to cup my cheek. I expect anger. Disgust. Anything but the mix of awe and concern in his eyes. "You cut your hair."

Unable to answer—or breathe—I swallow hard.

His fingers slide through the short strands, and his lips

curve gently. "I'd tell you I love it—because I do—but it doesn't matter what I think. You're the only person you have to answer to now."

Wyatt pushes to his feet, holds out his hand, and helps me up.

"I made such a mess..." I hate how small my voice is. "Give me a few minutes and I'll clean it up."

One eyebrow lifts slightly. "Hope, did you think I'd be angry? At the haircut or the mess?"

I can only nod.

"There's only one thing you could ever do that would make me angry." Careful not to step in the pile of hair on the floor, he leans closer. Twining our fingers, he squeezes gently. "Hide who you are. Or who you want to be. As long as you're true to yourself—whatever that means—I'll be happy."

"I don't know who I am anymore." The truth breaks down the wall I built around my heart three years ago. Shaking, I stagger back against the counter and cover my face with my hands. There aren't any tears. I'm not sad. Not scared. I'm numb.

"Hope. Look at me. Please." Wyatt keeps his tone gentle, and he doesn't move—not that I can see him in my current position. "What do you need from me? Space? Breakfast? Hell, I'll dance naked on the balcony if that'd help."

The idea of Wyatt dancing—let alone naked and in full view of the street—is so ridiculous, I drop my hands and offer him a weak smile. "You wouldn't."

"Try me." He strips off his Henley, turns, and heads for the French doors.

Racing after him, I catch him with one foot out on the balcony and his belt buckle undone. "If you're going to dance naked, you're doing it in the bedroom. For my eyes only."

Abject relief washes over him as goosebumps cover his

torso. "Thank fuck. It's colder than I thought it would be out here."

I trail my fingers over his chest, tracing the line of shrapnel scars down his side. Until my stomach growls loudly. "Put your shirt back on. For now. We can have a dance party after we eat."

ANY HOPE of getting naked disappears not long after we devour a stack of pancakes and try to figure out what we need to order from the grocery store.

Wyatt's phone rings, and he frowns as he taps the screen. "Ry? You're on speaker."

"Need you to come upstairs. West, Rip, and Inara are here too. Got some updates."

"We'll be up in ten minutes—"

"Just you for now."

I hold up my hand to stop Wyatt from saying something less than polite. "Excuse me? I'm the one Simon wants. And I'm the only one who knows how he operates. You are *not* leaving me out of this."

"Cara is on her way to you," Ryker says. "Rip's wife. She's going to take your new ID photos. We have a decent picture of Wyatt to use. We need one of you. Afterwards—"

"That's going to take all of five minutes. Try again." I'm shaking, three years of anger and frustration I wasn't allowed to express begging to be released. "I'm a mess. I admit it. But I'm not fragile."

"Never said you were," Ryker barks.

"Oh, fudgsicles. Give me the phone," Wren says. After a beat, the sound changes, and I think I hear a door close. "Hope, I'm sorry. Sometimes Ry forgets that not *everyone* works for him. Or thinks like he does. I'm on my way down too. The guys and Inara will review the intel they've gathered on Simon and his operation so far while you and I go through everything on that memory card. Divide and conquer. Okay?"

She sounds so logical. And honest. I want to believe her. But being too trusting is what got me into this mess. "Wouldn't it be better if I were up there?"

"Most of the briefing will be the intel you gave us yesterday. And as soon as we get all the financial horsepucky sorted out, we'll go back upstairs and join the rest of the team."

I meet Wyatt's gaze. He takes the phone and taps the mute button. "I won't let anyone sideline you, darlin'. Wren knows her shit. And if you need me, you know where I'll be."

I nod, and he hands me the phone. "I'll see you in a few minutes, Wren."

WYATT AND MURPHY HEAD UPSTAIRS, and I start a kettle of hot water. If I have any more coffee, I'll come out of my skin, and I doubt Wren wants anything caffeinated. The cabinets are surprisingly well stocked, and I find a box of chamomile apple tea that smells like heaven.

And a jar of gourmet honey.

The knock at the door isn't unexpected, but it still sends my heart rate shooting up. It doesn't help that the kettle goes off seconds later. As soon as I turn off the heat, I hurry over to the intercom. "Wren?"

"It's Cara. I'm Ripper's wife. I'm supposed to say 'firefly.'"

Wyatt's code.

The brunette standing in the hallway wears a nervous smile and, in her hands? A casserole that smells like everything good in the world. "I sent a pan with Ripper too, but this one's all ours."

Lasagna. It's been forever since I've had lasagna. Cheese.

Carbs. And oh, God. Is that sausage? We only had breakfast an hour ago, but I don't care.

I wave her inside, but before I can shut the door, the elevator dings, and I freeze. It's probably Wren. Right? Indecision keeps me frozen until I see her red hair. The relief sends a shudder all through me.

"Are you okay, Hope?" Cara asks, coming up behind me.

I stifle my yelp. "Shit. Sorry."

"Sorry for what?" Wren presses her hand to the small of her back. "Spitsnacks. This kid is going to be a soccer player. Or a kickboxer."

Spitsnacks?

"Lasagna? Cara, you read my mind!" With a little squeal, Wren half walks, half waddles over to the counter, peels back the foil, and breathes deeply. "I could eat this for every meal."

"Some days, you do," Cara says with a chuckle. "I make six pans at a time!"

Seeing the two women laugh with one another makes me long for my former life. The one before Simon. When I had friends.

Wren turns back to me, and her green eyes widen. "You changed your hair."

Touching the short, uneven strands, I stare down at my feet. At the boots that still bear a few bloodstains. "Simon liked it long."

"It's fabulous," she says. "Cara? Want to take the pictures for Hope's driver's license and passport? I'll get the plates."

15

Wyatt

RYKER'S top floor unit is equal parts command center and cozy living space. Large computer screens fill up the entire south wall, but on the other side of the room, two love seats flank a small table with a view over the whole city. Boxes with bright red flowers line the windows, and a bassinet stands in the corner, though the mattress is still wrapped in plastic.

A small, white dog runs up to Murphy and yips happily. "That's Pixel. She's...hyper," Ry says. "Probably should have walked her twice this morning."

The two circle one another, doing the standard butt-sniffing-get-to-know-each-other routine all dogs love. And then Pixel darts off to the corner, grabs a stuffed, squeaky lamb toy and drops it at Murphy's feet.

My best friend glances up at me, and I swear he's asking me for permission to *play*.

Shit. He's always been so focused. Five years together, and he's only ever played with those damn rawhide bones. My damage hasn't only affected me. It also doomed him to a life without anyone—or any other dogs—around. "Off duty," I say quietly.

Seconds later, he's rolling on the floor with the toy in his mouth while Pixel pounces on him.

West perches on a stool at a long counter, scrolling through information on his tablet. Inara's on the phone, her voice too low for me to hear, but she gives me a quick wave and disappears down the hall.

"She'll be back," Ryker says. "Her guy's on a business trip. Coffee's in the kitchen. Pull up a stool and get comfortable. We're gonna be here a while."

As I'm pouring a full mug, someone knocks.

"Come on in, brother. Cara down with Hope and Wren?" Ryker asks.

"Yeah." The voice isn't familiar, but there are only two men in the world Ryker would call "brother." Dax Holloway and Jackson "Ripper" Richards.

Ripper's shoulders hunch as he darts a gaze in my direction. At his side, a German Shephard with a mangled ear is on full alert.

Murph drops the toy and stares at me until I nod, signaling it's okay for him to relax.

Ry steps between us, tension gathering between his brows. "Rip..."

"It's nothing." The man leans down and rubs the German Shephard's good ear, then whispers something to him. Whatever it is, the dog relaxes, but doesn't leave Ripper's side.

"Wyatt Blake." I offer my hand, and after a beat, Rip stands.

"I don't..." His fingers flex around the strap of his laptop bag.

Fuck. I'm an idiot.

I shove my hand back into my pocket. "Stupid custom anyway."

Some of the strain on Rip's face eases, and he heads for

the long counter where he sets up his laptop, then gets himself a mug of coffee and parks himself on a stool next to me. "Heard about you," he says quietly. "I owe you. Everything."

It takes me a full minute to get over my shock enough to stammer out a reply. "We're...uh...square."

As soon as Inara joins us, her dusky cheeks redder than when she left, Ryker clears his throat.

"Wren and Hope are going over the intel on the memory card she stole from Arrens. They'll be up in a couple of hours. He's into some fucked-up shit, and Hope doesn't need to hear all of it."

"Hold up." Frustration crawls up my spine and bands around the back of my head. "We're not leaving Hope out of this. About anything. She had her choices taken away for three years. There's no fucking way I'm keeping things from her now."

Across the counter from me, Ripper straightens. "You're sure she can handle it?"

"No. But I'm damn sure she can't handle being kept in the dark. She lived with the asshole for three years. He beat the shit out of her if she said one wrong word. Controlled every part of her life—if you can even call what she had with him a life." The haunted look in Ripper's eyes warns me I'm about to cross a line.

"Enhanced interrogation. Indoctrination. Brainwashing. Torture. The bastard was so good at it, Rip forgot his own goddamn name."

West was careful not to go into detail about what Ripper went through, but the little he did say was enough for me to know I need to back off. Redirect if possible.

Scanning the room, I find exactly what I need. "Wait. Where are Graham and...you have another woman on the team, right?"

"Raelynn," West says. "She's on her way. Got a flat tire.

Graham's taking Q to a physical therapy appointment. We'll fill him in later."

Some of the darkness shrouding Ripper's gaze eases, and I sink back down onto the stool. My hip aches, and I caught my shoulder—and the fresh stitches—on the bathroom door jamb this morning. "So, everyone agrees? I won't keep anything from Hope."

Ry cracks his knuckles one at a time. "Your call, Wyatt. You trust her?"

If Ryker didn't have almost six inches on me, I'd lay him out flat for that comment. West sets down his tablet, his wiry muscles tensing. The two of us might have gone through BUD/S together, but he and Ryker are family. The kind forged through fire and blood.

"I trust her," I grit out. "And if you question her again—"

Another knock at the door, and the intercom crackles. "Y'all gonna let me in? I've had a day, and it ain't even noon yet."

If the woman on the other side of the door isn't from Texas, I'll eat Murphy's collar.

Raelynn is the textbook definition of fierce. Blond hair pulled up into a tight ponytail, full lips pressed into a thin line, flushed cheeks, and bright blue eyes. "What kind of bassackwards idiot spills a whole box of nails in the bike lane and just *leaves* the damn things there?"

She dumps a bike helmet and backpack on the floor, walks right up to me, and gives me the once over. "Where's your girl?"

"Downstairs. You...*biked* here? From where?"

"Can we get back to the briefing?" Ryker asks. "Or are we having a party?"

West clears his throat. "Raelynn, grab some coffee and take a seat. We're gonna be here a while."

WHILE RIPPER STARES intently at his laptop screen, West and Ryker debate the team's next move.

"If Arrens has a second in command—beyond that big dumbfuck I *disposed of* yesterday—he'll already be looking for Wyatt and Hope. That drone was broadcasting the whole damn time. Until it died," West says. "He's seen them together. The operator assured him Wyatt wouldn't live to see another sunrise, and Hope would regret the day she was born."

Despite not wanting to keep anything from Hope, I'm glad she's still with Wren and Cara. I'll be able to be gentle when I fill her in.

Gentle? You don't do gentle, remember?

Ripper rubs the back of his neck with a heavy breath. It's a gesture I've seen Ryker do more than once. The two of them share so many of the same mannerisms, through Ripper's are subdued, like he's desperate to blend in and just doesn't know how. "The guy who came after you was Brix Deeds. He has a brother. Rex. Bigger, meaner, and arrested three times for sexual assault in his early twenties. But he was never tried. All charges dismissed." Rip taps a few keys on his laptop and swears under his breath. "Because all of the victims disappeared. Probably his brother's doing. Looks like both of them were already working for Arrens at the time."

Fuck me.

West pours another cup of coffee. The man drinks it like water. "Safe to say he'll send Rex wherever he thinks Wyatt and Hope got off to. Since he knows Hope was heading over the pass, I don't see a scenario where they don't come to Seattle. And soon. Unless Arrens has another day he thinks he can get to her."

My anxiety spikes, turning my hands clammy, and a tight knot forms in my chest. I need to see Hope. To know she's okay. It doesn't matter that she's in a secured building with cameras, alarms, and the most overprotective bunch of men I've ever met. She's not with *me*. Murphy presses himself to my calves, and I reach down and scratch behind his ears. He knows. He always knows when I need him.

Ripper's dog, Charlie, sits next to the computer genius with his head on the man's thigh, and if I'm honest with myself, being in this room with these guys? It's the most "normal" I've felt in three years. Outside of the time I've spent with Hope.

If we stayed...

The idea that I could be a part of something again? It's really fucking tempting. But how the hell can I live here? In a city. With all the traffic and noises and people?

Along with grocery stores, restaurants, movie channels.

And Hope.

The din of conversation dies down, and from the look on Ripper's face, they're waiting for me to answer a question I didn't hear. "Sorry. What?"

"You okay?" West asks. "You're in another world."

"Yeah." Shaking off thoughts of what could be, I refocus on the men around me. "You're gonna have to repeat the question."

"Wasn't a question," Ryker says. "Arrens will probably send a team to Seattle. But that can't be his end game. This is a big goddamn city. What the hell does he expect to do? Go door to door for the next year?"

"He'll have a backup plan." West nods at Ripper. "Tell Wyatt what he missed while he was daydreaming."

Rip's hand goes to the back of his neck once more, and Charlie settles closer to him. "Hope fell off the grid three years ago. But digital footprints live forever." One corner of his mouth twitches. "Unless we get to them."

"What digital footprints?" I ask.

"Hope's emails. Phone logs. Financial records. It's a safe bet Arrens has all of this information. He's probably had it the whole damn time. But in case he doesn't, we're going to make it go away."

"I don't understand." Ripper won't meet my gaze, and unlike the rest of Ryker's team, I can't read him.

"Hope Raines has to disappear," Ryker says from across the room. "Until we can take out Arrens' whole crew—at least him and the top level generals—she can't contact anyone she knows. Can't even *think* about it."

"The whole crew? How many people are we talking here?" I ask.

Ryker nods at the tablet in front of me. Shit. Simon's entire organization is laid out on the screen. Thirty-two names. Eight directly under Simon—seven now that Brix is dead—and the rest...

"Simon has people everywhere."

I push the tablet away. "This isn't all of them. What about the cops? FBI agents? The assholes who run his brothels?"

"If we take out the top levels," West says, "the grunts will likely scatter to the winds without more than a gentle suggestion they'd live longer that way."

"And what about Hope? You really think this keeps her safe? If we miss even *one* of these assholes, they could come after her."

West frowns and Ryker pushes to his feet like they expect me to go batshit over their next words. This should be fun.

"We have to make it look like Simon and his men found Hope in Seattle and killed her. Give her a new name, fresh start, all that shit," West says.

I'm off the stool like someone lit it on fire. "She escaped so she could get her goddamn life back, and you want to take it away—"

Ryker growls an oath, but West claps him on the shoulder with one hand and slaps the other against the center of my chest. "Stand down, Ry. I've got this." Turning to me, the former SEAL holds my gaze. "Arrens treated her like she was nothing. Outside of what she could do for him—keep his books and be a convenient target for his anger—she said he barely spoke to her, right?"

My rage is a physical presence—growing by the second—and I stalk over to the window, Murphy on my six like glue. "She was alone. All the time."

Trapped in that huge house. Locked in when he wanted to punish her.

"Then do you really think anyone else in that organization would give her a second thought if they found out she was dead? She wouldn't have to disappear. Just change her last name and lie low for a month or two. Once Arrens is dead, no one else is going to scour the streets of Seattle trying to find her."

Holy shit.

West is right. Turning back to the group, I wonder if we really could have a life here. Until another thought shoves everything else from my head. "What about the trafficking ring? All his contacts in Mexico and Canada. The coyotes who bring in the victims. We can't let them ruin any more lives."

West, Ryker, and Inara exchange knowing glances. Even Ripper chuckles. Raelynn sidesteps me with her empty coffee mug and mutters something that sounds suspiciously like, "Hot damn. A new probie."

"We?" Ry asks. "You saying you want to stick around for a while? Help us out at Hidden Agenda?"

Shit. Do I? These men and women understand me in a way no one else can. And if I stayed...Hope and I could try for a life together.

Suddenly, the idea of spending another second away from her makes my skin crawl. I know she's with Wren and Cara. Only two floors away. In a building with more security than the fucking White House. But we're talking about taking her life away. Even if only for a few months.

"Maybe. I need to talk to Hope. Can we table this now? For

the night? I know she and Wren were supposed to join us, but..."

"Go back to her," West says. "There's not much more we can do until we flag and tag every single member of the organization. Learn their patterns, habits, weaknesses."

"That's gonna happen somewhere else." Ryker pulls out his phone and glances at the screen. "Wren's headed back up. She's tired. The rest of you can go to the warehouse or work from Rip's place. Just keep me in the loop."

West chuckles as he slides his tablet into a small backpack. "Never thought I'd see the day Ryker McCabe 'took a break.'"

"Did I say *I* was going to rest?" He arches his brows, one of them distinctly lower than the other and bisected by a thick scar. "I'm going to call in a favor. See if I can get any information about the fibbies on his payroll."

16

Hope

My shoulders ache, and after three hours bent over Wren's laptop reliving all the work I did to hide Simon's illegal activities, I'm wiped out.

I run my fingers through my hair, and despite my exhaustion, a smile tugs at my lips. Cara helped me clean it up in back, then took a few pictures for my new ID.

I'm Hope Hastings now. For how long, I'm not sure. Maybe forever.

Not all of our time was spent working to take down Simon and his organization, though. We sat out on the patio drinking tea, the two women helped me choose a week's worth of new clothes online, and when the packages were delivered an hour ago, we took a break so I could change into something that felt more like *me*.

The dark blue yoga pants, asymmetrical black sweater, and Keds give me the confidence I've lacked since I met Simon. I'm comfortable in my own skin—at least for a few minutes at a time. Until I remember how much danger we're in.

The door locks disengage, and I freeze on my way to the kitchen. My heart races until Murphy bounds into the apartment.

"What's wrong, darlin'?" Wyatt's deep voice soothes my raw nerves, but it's his embrace I've been craving since the moment he left.

I wind my arms around his waist and melt against him. "Today was just...a lot."

"You tell me what you need, and I'll give it to you." Being close to him chases away my fears. Strong fingers dig into my ass. He wants me. I can feel just how much when he pulls me closer.

"You." Tipping my head back, I stare up at him. He's tense. His lips bend into a frown, and the exhaustion in his eyes mirrors my own. "But...maybe we should sit? Or I could heat up some of the lasagna Cara brought over."

Wyatt dips his head and kisses me for all I'm worth. My back hits the wall—gently—and I drape my arms around his neck. The man kisses with his entire being. With so much passion it borders on desperation.

"Bedroom," he whispers against my cheek. "I want—I *need* —you naked."

With a little jump, I wrap my legs around his hips, and he carries me down the hall and into our room.

Our room.

Even if it can only be *ours* for a week or a day or the next few hours, I'll take it. I'll take any time I can have with him.

He lays me out on the bed, then stares down at me like he's seeing me for the first time. "You went shopping?" Fear lends an edge to his tone. "You left the building?"

"No!" I scramble back on the bed, pointing to the delivery boxes stacked neatly next to the closet. "We bought everything online. It was delivered. Cara went to pick up the boxes. Don't be angry—"

His jaw drops open, and his expression shifts. Horror. Regret. Sorrow. Wyatt spins on his heel and rushes from the room. "Murph. Leash." Thirty seconds later, the front door slams, and the two of them are gone.

Shit. He wasn't mad. He was scared. And I drove him away.

My cell phone dings faintly. I left it on the coffee table—I think. Tears lend a shimmer to the world as I retrieve it to find a single message.

I'm sorry.

No word on when he'll be back. No mention of where he's going. Just an apology when he didn't do anything wrong.

CARA UNCORKS a bottle of wine and pours two glasses. I cried for fifteen minutes after Wyatt left. Then called her. She and Wren are the only two people I know in this town—besides Ryker and West, and there's no way in hell I'm talking to a man about what just happened.

"Have you texted him back?" she asks. We curl up on the love seat with a view of Puget Sound spread out before us. After a sip of wine, I shake my head.

"I don't know what to say. He didn't do anything wrong—"

"Hold on." She sets her glass down and reaches for my free hand. "That's not entirely true."

"I'm the one who panicked. Who overreacted."

Her eyes soften. "You don't know me very well yet, but I was on the run when I met Ripper. Two JSOC agents—dirty ones—were trying to kill me. And Ripper was..." After a heavy sigh, she holds my gaze. "Most of it is his story to tell—one he'll probably never share with you—but he was tortured for a long time. Physically, but even more so, mentally."

My cheeks flame red hot, and I stare down at my knees. "West told us he was brainwashed until he didn't remember who he was. Or...West told Wyatt. He still thought Ripper was dead."

"Oh," Cara says softly. "That...was probably for the best. He doesn't talk about it with anyone but me and the guys."

Regret raises a lump in my throat. "I'm sorry. I won't tell him I know."

"I will." After she squeezes my fingers again, she sits back. "This family doesn't keep secrets. We've all been burned by them." Silence stretches between us until Cara shakes her head. "Sorry. That turned dark in a hurry, didn't it?"

"A little. But my life has been pretty dark the past few years. I get the sense Wyatt's has too. Even though he hasn't told me much about what happened when he left the SEALs."

"He will. When he's ready. Like you'll tell him more about what you went through. Trust takes time. Even when you love one another."

Love? I choke on a sip of wine, barely keeping it from shooting out my nose.

"I can see it when you talk about him. Wren did too. And she can spot two people who should be together from a mile away. Or over a video call. It's happened more than once the past couple of years."

"Oh, *that* is a story I need to hear." It feels good to laugh, despite how worried I am about Wyatt.

Cara sobers, her fingers fluttering around the stem of her wine glass. "You were triggered, Hope. Given what you went through, it will probably happen a lot. At least for a while. And Wyatt knows he's the one who triggered you. So he's going to feel guilty. That's okay."

"But..."

Cara's eyes glisten, almost as if she's about to cry. "If I touch Ripper the wrong way—even by accident—his mind goes right back to his time in Turkmenistan with that...sadistic piece of shit who almost killed him. We've been together two years now, and it still happens occasionally. I never do it on purpose, but I feel guilty every time." She rises and moves to the French doors. "Can I open these for a minute?"

"Sure." Joining her, I breathe in the fresh air and stare down at the street below. Is that...?

It is.

Wyatt and Murphy head for the south corner of the block, turn, and disappear. Has he been doing laps this whole time?

At my side, Cara pats her cheeks, and the bright red tinge to them fades. "It took me a long time—and a lot of therapy—to understand that my guilt isn't misplaced or wrong. It's *normal.* But it's not okay for me to beat myself up for making a mistake. There's a difference. Wyatt's apology? That was one hundred percent the right thing for him to do."

"And him doing laps around the block for the past half an hour?" I point to the north side of the street where the two round the corner.

"That's him beating himself up." She smiles, but her eyes are still sad. "So text him. Tell him you were triggered, but you're okay now. Tell him to come home. I'll stay with you until he does."

Ten minutes later, he still hasn't responded. We're back on the couch, our wine glasses empty. "So what are you and Wyatt going to do once this whole mess is over?" Cara asks. "Will you stay? Ryker doesn't let anyone live in this building he doesn't trust. So it's quiet. Safe. Secure."

Sinking back against the cushions, I chew on my lower lip. We've only been here for twenty-four hours, but this apartment already feels like it could be home. But I lived in L.A. I love big cities. After the isolation of the past three years, I crave the bustle. Even the people.

"Hey? What's wrong?" Cara leans closer, concern in her eyes. "I didn't mean to pry."

"No, it's not that." Staring out at the city, I run a hand through my hair. I'm free now. Wearing clothes that are mine. With a man who talks to me. Who listens to me. Who doesn't yell or hit or punish me for every single word I say. A man who risked his life for me. "Wyatt hates it here."

"So did Ripper."

"What?" At her nod, I ask, "Then why are you living here?"

"Because this is where Ry is. And this is where he met me. He's learned how to manage his fear. But it's still hard for him some days. For me too."

"I wish we could find a compromise. A way to live here but still find the peace Wyatt needs."

Cara's eyes gleam, and she reaches over to pat my thigh. "Give him a little time. He might realize peace and quiet are as much about who you're with as where you are."

Wyatt

The sun lost its battle with the stars almost an hour ago. I stopped counting our laps around the block after number fifteen. My hip is on fire, the bone-deep ache making every step pure agony.

Murphy thinks this is the greatest thing since his rawhide bone. I swear he's actually prancing. Gotta find a dog park tomorrow. Or some place for him to run.

Me? I could sleep for a week. Before I met Hope, I spent my days working from dawn to dusk. Chopping wood, fishing, hunting. Some times, Murphy and I would just...walk. Pick a direction and hike until the sun was high in the sky, then turn around and come home.

It's the stress. The constant worry Simon's going to find her. And about a million pounds of guilt.

"I'm sorry too. I know you weren't mad at me. You were worried. I'm okay. Come home."

I stare at the text message for the tenth time as Murphy finds another tree to mark. "Coward," I mutter under my breath. "She needed you, and you *left her*."

Come home.

Not come back. *Come home*.

Fuck. "Time to go, pal." Winding Murphy's leash around my palm, I meet his gaze, then jerk my head toward the building's front doors. "We've been hiding long enough."

Hope and Cara are sitting on the love seat when I code myself back into the unit. Murphy goes right to his favorite corner and starts gnawing on his bone. Hope's shoes are by the door. Cara's too. There's nothing else personal in the space—not yet—but it's still starting to feel like we belong here. Like...a home.

"I should get back to Rip," Cara says. "You know where I am if you need anything." The two women hug, and from the look on Hope's face, they're fast on their way to becoming friends. If not already there.

Once we're alone, I shove my hands into my pockets. "I shouldn't have snapped at you."

"And I shouldn't have assumed you were angry," she says quietly. "But it's going to happen sometimes. Like your nightmares. We can't control what triggers us."

"Can I hold you?" Those four words shouldn't be so hard to say, but I have to force each one out over the lump in my throat.

Tears glisten in her eyes. I'm terrified she's going to say no until she rushes to me and wraps her arms around my waist.

"There's so much I want to say to you, darlin'. But..."

Hope meets my gaze, and one of those tears spills over and

trails down her cheek. "We have time, Wyatt. Just...don't run away from me again."

"I wasn't running from you." Catching the tear with my thumb, I dash it away. "I was running from myself. From my own feelings. I'm just so damn scared I'm going to hurt you and you'll never trust me again."

She cups the back of my neck and guides me until our foreheads touch. "Then promise me one thing. If you get scared again, tell me. Don't run without telling me why."

"That I can do."

LYING in bed with Hope in my arms? It feels so right. Over dinner, I filled her in on what Ryker's team is planning. She was quiet after that, only coming out of her shell for brief moments —mostly when Murphy demanded she throw his tennis ball or scratch behind his ears.

"What do *you* want, Wyatt?" she asks, her voice quiet. Small. Afraid. "After this is all over."

With the blackout curtains drawn, it's completely dark in the room, but when I relax my hold on her, she turns over so we're face to face.

"I want to be with you, darlin'. But even more...I want you to be happy. If you need time alone to heal? I'll leave. Go back to my cabin and install a phone line so you can reach me any time. Day or night. Or I'll move into the unit next door so I'm close but not...here. Whatever you need from me, you'll have. I promise."

"You're too good to be true." She trails her fingers over my chest, and I'm hard for her in less than ten seconds. "If I...*died*— if Wren and Ripper made Hope Raines disappear forever— would I have to find a new career? Be someone totally different?

Could I ever contact my old friends? Or...try to reconcile with my mom?"

"We—Ryker's team—are taking down the whole ring. Simon, all of his generals. And they'll shut down the brothels too." I brush a kiss to her forehead. "The grunts aren't going to look for you. They'll find some other asshole to work for and forget all about you—if they even knew about you in the first place. As long as you don't plan on running for public office or becoming a movie star, you could still work in finance. And we could arrange a trip for you to talk to your mom. Might need to bring some extra security along, but..."

"I'll do it." Snuggling closer, she drapes her arm over me. I can *feel* her tension melting away. "I want to be free."

"You are free, darlin'. And I'm going to make damn sure you stay that way."

17

Hope

"THIS IS SAFE, RIGHT?" I ask. "Leaving the building?"

At the breakfast bar, Wyatt slides our tablets and a handful of granola bars into a messenger bag. "It's safe, darlin'. I promise."

"How can you be so sure?" Zipping up my soft purple hoodie, I stare at the leather holster clipped to Wyatt's belt. I was fine until he pulled the gun from the safe. Now, my stomach is one big ball of nerves, and I can't stop my hands from shaking.

"Because Ry's bringing Wren." With a smile, Wyatt snags his canvas jacket from the back of one of the bar stools and shrugs into it. "You saw the two of them together. If there was *any* risk, we'd probably hear them arguing from down here."

"I got an earful when we were going over the files on the memory card. I guess she had an appointment for a pedicure the other day, and Ryker wouldn't let her go alone. He sat in the chair next to her the whole time. Arms crossed, completely silent."

Wyatt laughs, and it changes his face so completely, I'm mesmerized. My first day with him, his frown lines were etched so deep, they looked like they'd been carved in granite. In the past few days, he's started to relax. Like maybe...he could be happy here.

"I'd pay to see that," he says. "The man doesn't own a single piece of clothing that isn't black. I bet he glared at every single customer."

His hand lingers on mine as he passes me a travel mug full of coffee. Every touch sends a little thrill through me. He's so tender, but in some ways, I think he's more possessive than Ryker.

The mug goes into the side pocket of my purse. Emotion clogs my throat, and I turn away. I didn't realize how important something as simple as owning a purse—and a wallet—could be. I cried as I filled the bag with lipstick, a brand new clutch wallet, and my very own key card for *our* apartment.

Wrapping me in his embrace, Wyatt presses a gentle kiss to my forehead. "If you need a break today, if it's too much at any time, if *anyone* triggers you, tell me. Okay?"

"I'll be fine." His brows furrow, and I swear he almost growls. "I have to be, Wyatt. Because this is how I get my life back."

Half an hour later, Ryker parks in front of a large warehouse. It looks like any other industrial building in any other city—except for the rather odd mix of cars in the lot. And the woman carrying a road bike on her shoulder as she heads for a metal door directly in front of us.

"I pay her enough she could buy a car," Ryker mutters as he helps Wren down from the front seat. The petite redhead braces a hand at the small of her back and stares up at him.

"Not everyone is you, Ry."

His right eyebrow arches. "Of course not. I'm one of a kind, little bird. Mean and ugly enough they broke the mold. Good thing too. Otherwise you'd have two of me to deal with." His deadpan delivery and the complete lack of humor in his expression makes Wren laugh, which I think might have been the point.

"Snickerdoodles. I can barely handle one of you. Though an extra babysitter *would* come in handy in a couple of months."

Ripper—who didn't say a single word the entire drive—pulls a duffel bag from the back of the massive SUV. His German Shepherd, Charlie, is glued to his side. "Cara can't wait to be an aunt," he says quietly. "You won't be hurting for help."

Wren grins at me and Wyatt. "I hope not. Though Cara's going to need backup."

Is she talking about us? Wyatt takes my hand, his grip almost painfully tight.

"All that shrapnel damage...the docs don't think I can have kids."

Did he want them? Before Simon, I'd thought maybe... But after the hell of the last three years, I'm not even sure if I can take care of myself, let alone a child.

Ripper shuts the back hatch of the SUV, and I jerk back to reality. Wondering about what might have been or might never be? That can wait until Ryker's team stops Simon.

"Wow." A massive climbing wall rises at least fifty feet in the air along one side of the warehouse. Next to it, a boxing ring, free weights, and several machines I don't recognize, but that look...painful.

The far corner is almost homey. A kitchen, dining table,

couches, recliners, gaming consoles, ping pong and foosball tables, even thick, blue carpets.

Wren shuffles off to one of the recliners, swivels it around to face a big conference table next to a huge wall of computer equipment, and sinks down with a sigh. "Make yourself comfortable, Hope. Drinks are in the fridge, snacks are in the cabinet. MREs…well, I don't recommend those much."

"Looks a hell of a lot different than the last time I was here." Wyatt drops the messenger bag on one of the couches and rubs his fingers over the rough stubble on his chin. Wandering over to the boxing ring, he runs his hand along the padded ropes. "Still have workouts twice a week?"

From the kitchen, where he's starting a pot of coffee, West snorts. "Three times. At least. Four if even a single thing went wrong on our last op."

Wyatt chuckles. "Sounds about right. This setup makes me wish I'd kept my boxing gloves."

"Got plenty of gear in the lockers." Filling a metal water bottle, West nods toward the back of the warehouse. "You want to go a few rounds, we'll make it happen."

"Hey. I'm Raelynn." The tall, willowy blond with a thick Texas accent strides over to me and thrusts out her hand. Her firm grip matches her stance—back ramrod straight, shoulders set. If there's a single ounce of fear in this woman, it's buried so deep, no one will ever find it.

"Hope. But I guess you could figure that out."

"Met everyone yet?" she asks.

I shake my head. "Wyatt has, I think. But I haven't."

"So, here's the deal. I was Air Force for ten years. Inara over there? She's a sniper. Former Army Ranger. Graham was in the Coast Guard. You came in with Ripper, so assumin' you met him already. He can trace a single dollar all the way to hell and back again. West plans all our shit, and Ryker rides our asses the whole damn time."

"Where's Caleb?" West asks.

Ryker runs a hand over his bald head. "I didn't tell him about today. Something's off with that one. Wren's working on a fresh background packet. When she's done, we'll decide what to do with him."

"Sure you don't want Zephyr to 'check my work'?" Wren mutters.

"Baby, that's not why I asked her for help." In three steps, Ryker's in front of Wren. He drops to a knee and tries to take her hand, but she keeps her gaze pinned to her laptop screen. "You couldn't stop throwing up. You needed to rest."

Everyone looks away as Ryker slides Wren's laptop aside and wraps her in his arms. He murmurs to her, his deep voice too low to make out the words, and when he stops, Wren sniffles once, then clears her throat. "Can we get to work, please?"

"Right. Hope?" Ryker pushes to his feet. "We need a list of everyone you knew before you met Arrens. Friends. Family. Anyone you were close to. Wren's going to track them down and we'll find some locals we can trust to keep an eye on them."

Shock makes my stomach pitch. Would Simon really go after my friends? Of course he would. "There aren't many. A couple of people from my last job at Angel City Financial Services. My college roommate. One woman I've known since grade school. And...my mom. But I haven't talked to her since I graduated high school."

Six people—plus a former coworker whose last name I can't remember. The sum total of my life before Simon. How did I let myself get so isolated? I chatted with the regulars at my yoga class. The barista at my local coffee shop—Agnes—knew me by name. But true friends? The kind of friends who know all of your secrets? Who are always there for you? I'm not sure I even had one.

I lean against Wyatt on the couch, Murphy's head in my lap. Ripper sits ten feet away, and every few minutes, another photo of one of Simon's top-level generals appears on the giant monitor on the wall.

"Each picture gets uploaded to Wren's facial recognition software," West explains. "Once she hacks into Salt Lake City's traffic camera network, we can track them any time they're in public."

"If they aren't wearing overly large sunglasses, hats, or face masks," Ripper adds without looking up from his keyboard.

Oh. Great.

"How the hell do you expect to find them if it's that easy to confuse a facial recognition program?" Wyatt asks. He's so tense, his muscles are rigid.

"Traffic cameras are only *one* way we track these assholes." Ryker crosses his massive arms over a chest that goes on for miles and glares at us. He might be the most intimidating man I've ever seen. If he confronts Simon, my abuser is going to shit his pants. "We tag their credit cards. Phones. Parents. Kids. Friends. In under twenty-four hours, we'll be so far up their asses, they won't be able to sit down for a week."

Wyatt

Watching Ryker and his team work makes me long for the days I ran my own team. Between the serious shit—financial analysis, establishing surveillance at some of the smaller brothels, and tracking down Hope's former friends—they joke around, take short stints on the climbing wall, even shoot hoops at the half-court in the far corner of the warehouse.

"Blowing off some steam helps concentration."

Never thought I'd hear those words coming from Ryker McCabe. The man fought his way out of Hell, then ran, stumbled, and crawled almost five miles down a fucking mountain.

And he wanted to go right back up again despite being unable to stand.

And now he "blows off steam"? What's next? Company picnics and a trust circle?

Hope and Raelynn play a quick foosball game after Wren decides she *needs* a pizza—with extra anchovies. Inara and Graham are on their way back with half a dozen large pies. Unsure what to do, I join Ryker in the kitchen.

"So," he says as the coffee pot starts to sputter, "you sticking around?"

"Jesus, Ry. Does that matter right now? Following the money is slow as fuck, two of Hope's friends are still unaccounted for, and we've been at this all day." Bracing my hands on the counter, I stare out the small window over the sink. The warehouse is a good ten miles from downtown. Tall buildings in the distance rise dramatically against a bright, blue sky. It's almost peaceful in a strange way.

"Hell yes, it matters. Look at her, Wyatt." Ryker doesn't move a muscle. Just stares at me while I turn my focus to Hope.

"Got one!" she cries and pumps her fist in the air. "Finally." Light dances in her eyes. This is her...happy. Relaxed.

As we worked today—as Ripper and Wren asked her questions about her life *before*, while the rest of us poured over detailed files on all of Simon's goons—her energy waned. More than once she reached for me or Murphy, close to tears.

And now, she's smiling. Laughing. West comes up behind her, whispers something in her ear, and she shoots him a wicked grin. Two seconds later, she scores another point.

"Givin' away all my secrets ain't playin' fair." Raelynn cracks her neck and hunkers down closer to the paddles. "All right, city girl. It's *on* now."

Ryker snags two bottles of water from the fridge and slides one across the counter to me. "It took me a long time to realize what I had here—what we *all* had here."

"A good team?"

His eyes—the oddest mix of blue, green, and hazel—narrow, and he shakes his head. "No, dumbass. A family. One we chose for ourselves. Everyone here pulls a salary, sure. But they'd be here anyway. Because that's what family does. We show up. No matter what. You can't tell me you don't miss that."

The admission shouldn't be so hard. Or cost so much. But I can't get the words out. Clenching my fists tight enough my knuckles crack, I fight against the overwhelming wave of emotion trying to pull me under. In the end, "Fuck," is all I can say.

Ry claps me on the shoulder briefly—the man's never been one for close, personal contact—before snagging his water bottle and cracking the seal. "So, that's a yes? I'll warn you now. Raelynn's gonna insist on calling you 'Probie.'"

"I can't leave Hope. No travel. Not unless—"

"No one's asking you to. If it's not safe, you can help run shit from here. Rip stays in Seattle. Always. Hell, I haven't even been on a mission in six months. Not since we found out about the baby."

I stare at the man, dumbfounded. Ryker McCabe doesn't "sit things out." But then Hope's laugh breaks through my shock, and I understand. Because there isn't one damn thing I wouldn't do for her.

I can't lie to myself any longer. I'm not falling for her. I'm in love with her. When we get home tonight—whether that apartment is just a temporary home or something much more permanent—I have to tell her.

"Pizza's here," Ry says with a quick nod toward the window. "I'll tell West you're in. We'll make it official once we know Hope's safe and Arrens is dead—"

"Fudgenuggets!" Wren snaps, sitting up so fast, all I see out of the corner of my eye is a red blur. "Everyone get over here. I'm going to project."

I run back to Hope, then wrap my arm around her waist as we face the big screen on the wall.

"I cracked the password on Hope's old email account," Wren says. Her voice doesn't waver, but she glances up at Ry. The man peers down at her laptop, and a muscle in his jaw starts pulsing rapid fire. "This was the most recent message."

I have been patient long enough, Hope. If you don't return to me within twenty-four hours, you won't like the consequences.

A rough sob tears from Hope's throat. Her knees buckle, and I pull her tighter to my side.

"There's more," Wren says quietly. "A video."

On screen, a woman cowers on the floor of a brightly lit room. Her gray dress is torn and bloody. Bruises cover her arms and legs. One eye is swollen shut.

"Bettina!" Hope cries. "No..."

A man's voice barks out an order. "Tell her! Now!"

"M-Miss H-Hope," the woman whispers. She's shaking so badly, she can barely speak. But as she peers up at the camera, her gaze hardens. "Don't come back—"

Three men surround the woman, kicking her from every angle. The camera doesn't capture their faces, but they're all big guys. Bettina curls into a ball, sobbing, until one of them catches her in the head, and she passes out.

"Let's play a game, Hope," a male voice says. "It's called 'Simon says.' It's simple. Simon says get your ass back here and *maybe* he'll let the bitch live."

The video stops, and Wren turns off the screen. "The time stamp on the email message is two hours ago. Ninety minutes *after* the FBI opened an official investigation based on the information on the memory card," she says.

"Son of a bitch." Ryker kicks a small plastic trash bin halfway to the boxing ring. "I'm calling Pritchard. And Connor. Whoever told Arrens about the investigation is going to regret the day they were born." He pulls out his phone and sweeps a gaze around the room. "Anyone who can't be wheels up in three hours better say something right fucking now."

No one says a word until Ripper stands. "Ry?"

"I know, brother. You're staying here."

Rip swallows hard and straightens his shoulders. "No. Not this time. I'm going with you."

18

Hope

RYKER'S TEAM is in constant motion. Packing weapons. MREs. Tech.

All I can do is sit on the couch, my arm around Murphy, and stare off into space.

Bettina risked her life for me. Without her, I never would have escaped. Never would have met Wyatt. Or Wren. Ryker. Cara.

I can't let Simon hurt any of them.

For five years, Bettina was trapped in one of Simon's brothels. He brought her to his compound six months before I moved to Salt Lake City. She's endured so much and she's not even thirty. He'll never let her go. But maybe if I do what he says, he won't kill her.

"Hope?" Wyatt kneels next to me. His hands shake as he runs them over my thighs. "You haven't said a word in almost an hour. Cara brought some clothes for us to take with us."

"Why?"

His brows furrow. "Because we're leaving as soon as the

plane's ready. The rest of the team has go bags here."

"I don't need clothes, Wyatt. Simon won't let me keep them."

He recoils like I've just slapped him. "What the fuck? You are *not* going back to that asshole!"

Murphy tenses. Ryker makes a beeline for us from across the warehouse. Great. *Two* alpha men about to tell me what I can and can't do.

"If I don't, he'll kill Bettina. She helped me escape. Without her, I never would have made it." Tears brim in my eyes, and I swipe at them with one hand. I can't seem to let go of Murphy. "At least I had a few days to remember what it's like to be free. To be...cared for."

"No," Wyatt growls. "I won't let you do this. You're staying here." He pushes to his feet with a groan, turns, and finds Ryker right behind him. "Hope isn't going with us."

"Yes, she is." Ry slaps a hand in the center of Wyatt's chest. "We need her. We know nothing about Simon's compound. The only blueprints Wren can find are more than ten years old, and the satellite images don't match the original construction."

"She. Stays. Here."

The two men stare one another down. Wyatt grabs Ry's hand and twists, but before I can blink, he's flat on his back, groaning. Ryker backs up two steps. The pure, raw anger in his multi-hued eyes would terrify me if I weren't about to go back to the man who made my life a living hell for three years.

"Your skills need serious work," Ryker says sharply. "Outside. Now. We're not doing this in front of her." He snaps his fingers. "Graham, get the fuck over here."

The younger man drops a stack of MREs and rushes across the warehouse like someone's chasing him. "What's wrong?"

"Hope thinks she's going back to Arrens. Tell her what we do here. I need to knock some sense into this asshole." Ryker grabs Wyatt's forearm and pulls him to his feet. "We'll be back."

Graham takes one look at me, then perches on the arm of the sofa. Murphy settles closer, though his gaze follows Ryker and Wyatt as they head for the side door.

"You don't have to babysit me." Running my fingers through Murphy's sleek coat, I blink away the tears burning my eyes. He won't understand why I'm not around anymore, and I wish I could explain it to him.

"You sure? Dinners on my watch are always pizza and mint chip ice cream." He cracks a smile, and it's so genuine, my own lips curve into a weak grin. "Hope, we're not just a team here. This is family." Graham unlocks his phone, stares at it for a moment, and holds it out to me. "That's my boyfriend, Q."

In the photo, Graham has his arm around a taller, skinnier man with light brown hair. They're laughing, and I think...that's West in the background. "You look happy."

"We are. But five months ago, his ex kidnapped him when I was on a training mission with the team." Graham frowns, and his shoulders hike up close to his ears. "Alec was certifiable. Literally. Anti-social personality disorder. The fucker didn't have the ability to feel guilt or remorse or sympathy. When he took Q...I was sure he was going to kill him. We didn't know where they were or even how long they'd been gone."

"But...he's okay now, right?"

The furrow between Graham's brows eases slightly. "He is. Because as soon as we realized he was missing, we got to work." He huffs, then shakes his head. "Well, everyone *else* got to work. I was useless until we had a plan."

"Why are you telling me this?" All I want to do is hold Murphy—and Wyatt—until I can't anymore. Try to memorize everything about them so I have a few happy memories to hold onto when my life is nothing but fear and pain. Until Simon eventually kills me.

"So you understand how good we are at what we do," Graham says. "Utah is the last place I ever thought I'd be going back to. That's where Alec took Q. Way out in the middle of nowhere." He shakes his head again and pockets his phone. "You're part of the family now—whether you want to be or not. And no one messes with this family and lives to brag about it."

Swallowing hard, I fight to find my voice. "I can't let you all risk your lives for me. Simon's compound is a fortress. Hell, it's probably more secure than the White House!"

A hint of a smile ghosts Graham's lips. "He'll never admit it —top secret, 'if I told you, I'd have to kill you' type shit—but I'm pretty sure West has run infil ops for the Secret Service more than once."

I gape at him. Even if that's true, how can he be so confident? Simon won't hesitate to kill anyone he thinks is helping me.

"Please don't do this. Take me to Salt Lake City, then let me go. For Q. And Cara. And Wren. I can't be responsible for anyone else getting hurt."

Murphy whines and nudges my chin as my tears spill over.

"Please..." I say again. "Ryker never should have asked any of you to risk your lives for me."

Graham slides off the arm of the couch and sits next to me. "You're not responsible for anything that asshole does. You never were." He turns his hand palm up on his thigh. "And Ry didn't ask. He never does." He wiggles his fingers. I need human connection more than anything right now, so I place my hand in his. "We're here because the world is full of bad people doing terrible things. And we can stop them."

He's so earnest, there's nothing I can say to convince him Simon's unstoppable. So I let him hold my hand while I stare at the rest of the team preparing to fight for my life.

Once we're back in Salt Lake City, I'll slip away. Somehow. After I make sure Wyatt won't follow me. A broken heart will heal. A shot to the head won't.

Wyatt

Ryker shoves me through the door and slams it behind us. "You want to fight? Take your best shot. But you better make it count because it's the only one you're gonna get." He holds out his arms. "Come at me."

My punch finds nothing but air.

"Thought so. You're so fucked in the head, you can barely see straight."

"Go to hell," I grit out.

He arches his brows. The left one rises a little less than the right. "Already been there. I don't plan on going back."

Shit. "That was..."

"Insensitive as fuck? Yeah. It was. So was talking to Hope the way you did. She just escaped *three years* of Arrens controlling her whole goddamn life, and you think barking orders at her was the way to go?"

I stumble back until I hit the metal wall. He's right. I treated Hope like she didn't matter. Like what she *wanted* didn't matter. "I have to talk to her."

Ry catches my arm before I reach the door and steers me toward the corner of the building. "Nope. Not yet. We're not done."

"I fucked up. I can't let her think I'd ever—"

"She doesn't." Rubbing his hand over his bald head, Ryker blows out a long, slow breath. "Hope's pissed off, but she knows you're protective as hell and twice as stubborn. You'll apologize, grovel some, and she'll forgive you. As long as you don't let it happen again."

For several seconds, I stare at him. "Don't let it happen again? She wants to *go back to that asshole!*"

"She wants to protect you. And the rest of us." He holds up his hand when I growl an oath. "Can you blame her?"

Until this moment, I thought Ryker McCabe was one of the smartest men I'd ever met. If I stood a chance, I'd beat some sense into him.

"Simon would lock her in a windowless room for *days* if she said one wrong word. Now that the feds are involved? He'll kill her. And Bettina."

"She knows that." Ry holds my gaze, and while he's standing right in front of me, a part of him isn't here. He's back in Hell. Or Russia when he almost lost Wren. Or on any number of missions all over the world with his team. "Hope's been alone for a long time. She doesn't understand what it's like to have a family."

This isn't a conversation I expected to have with Ryker, but as I stare at him, I see the truth in his eyes. "You do."

"Damn straight. And after we put an end to this pig fucker, you will too. You and Hope." He checks his watch. "We're leaving here in twenty minutes. If you want Cara to take Murphy, catch her before she leaves. I need to talk to Wren before we go."

"You're...going with us? What happened to 'I haven't been on a mission in six months'?"

"Dax and Ripper are both alive because you, West, and Inara found me when I broke out of Hell. So, yeah. I'm going with you. Got a problem with that?"

I'd hug him if either of us did that sort of thing. But we don't, so I shake my head. "Murphy can go with Cara. Just...let me say goodbye to him first." How the hell am I supposed to leave my best friend—my partner—behind? But this isn't Afghanistan. And Murph's been out of the field for more than three years. It's too dangerous.

"You're coming back," Ry says as he strides toward the door. "We're all coming back."

19

Wyatt

An hour into the flight to Salt Lake City and Hope hasn't said one word to me. She cried when she hugged Murphy. Then Cara and Wren. She's still convinced she's not coming back.

The private plane is nicer than any I've ever been on. A perk of the partnership Ryker and Dax formed last year.

Two rows of plush seats face each other with a large table in the middle, and West sketches the layout of Simon's compound on his tablet.

"The walls won't be a problem," he says. "We've scaled higher. What about the house itself?"

Hope leans forward, her elbows on her knees. The exhaustion in her eyes is killing me. I want to wrap her in my arms and carry her so far from Salt Lake City, that asshole will never find her.

But I can't. We have to stop him first.

"It's impenetrable." After a sigh, she runs her fingers through her dark hair. "Simon has this futuristic security system. It's...biologic—no—bio..."

"Biometric?" West asks. "The access control? We can blast right through any locks."

"No. I mean it scans anyone inside. Body weight, height, heart rate, respiration rate. He paid a fortune for it. Whenever anyone new showed up, Brix had to program them into the system." Her voice cracks, and I hand her a bottle of water. Hope's gaze collides with mine, and she mouths, *"Thanks."*

It's something.

"Then we'll hack it. Rip, call Cam if you need her help." West flips his tablet around so Hope can see the blueprints Wren found online. "We need to label each one of these rooms."

Ripper drums his fingers on his thighs. Graham pushes to his feet and strides to the back of the plane. A few seconds later, he drops down next to Rip and hands him a cup of coffee. "Drink this."

The change in him is almost immediate. His shoulders relax, and though his hands aren't steady when he accepts the steaming cup, the first sip centers him. "I'll be okay," he says, as much to himself as to Graham. "Forgot what it was like. On mission."

"You're not breaching with us," Ry says. "There's new construction not far from Simon's compound. Half a dozen houses still unfinished. You, Hope, and Wyatt are staying there while the rest of us take that asshole and his crew down."

My first instinct is to protest. I want to see Arrens take his last breath. Hell, I want to be the one to end him. But I won't leave Hope's side.

"Rip stays in Seattle. Always. Hell, I haven't even been on a mission in six months."

Ryker's words play on a loop in my head. Yet, he and Ripper are both here. Both ready to lose everything to save a woman they've only known for three days.

"There's no cell service," Hope says, the edge to her voice

drawing me back to the present. "Simon and his men all have special phones. One time, he had a repairman come to work on the dishwasher. I stole the guy's phone and tried to call for help, but it didn't work."

When she shudders and covers her face with her hands, I raise the armrest between us and pull her against me. "Deep breaths, darlin'. You're safe. He can't get to you here."

She jerks away. "We're on a plane, Wyatt. Of course he can't get to me *here*." After a blink, she curses under her breath. "There are at least six armed men around the compound all the time. Another six who travel with him. He's never alone. Never unprotected."

"Sounds a lot like Russia," Ry says. His expression darkens, and a muscle in his jaw ticks until he cracks his neck. "Kolya—piece of shit heroin kingpin—took Wren. He had dozens of men, cameras, and drug runners who kept watch and reported on anything suspicious. He died. Painfully. So will Simon."

THE SUN SETS outside the half-finished house in Salt Lake City, but we can't see it. Ryker tacked black plastic over every window, and battery-powered floodlights illuminate what will one day be a formal living room.

West unrolls a large piece of butcher paper and tapes it to the wall. Ten minutes later, he puts the finishing touches on a sketch of Simon's compound. Everything Hope could tell us down to the approximate measurements of all the rooms.

"It's likely Bettina is either in the basement or in the upstairs space, here." West points to the small, windowless room Simon would lock Hope in when he wanted to punish her. "Infil is going to be a bitch if we can't pinpoint her location."

"Working on it," Ripper says. On his laptop screen, the walls of the compound come into view. "Switching to thermals." After a few taps to his keyboard, the feed flickers, and turns black and green. A handful of red shapes move slowly on either side of the compound, but the center is nothing but a black void.

"Rip?" Ry peers over the tech genius's shoulder. "Is something wrong with the drone?"

A tremor racks Ripper's hand until he makes a fist. "No. The entire place is a dead zone." He directs the drone to fly in a wide 360 view of the house, garage, gardens, and outer walls, but nothing on screen changes. "Fuck!" He throws the joystick onto the makeshift table fashioned from plywood and sawhorses and pushes away. "Nothing but a fucking failure."

He's up the sweeping—but unfinished—staircase before anyone can stop him. Ry shoots West a hard stare. "Keep working. I'll talk to him."

Neither of the men make a sound on the stairs, and West carries on like nothing happened. Except for the strain in his voice. "Clearly, his signal jammers extend beyond the edge of the property. Blind infil is risky as fuck, but we've done it before. Huddle up. This is gonna get complicated."

Hope

The minutes pass slowly, despite the buzz of activity around me. A small speaker attached to some sort of satellite receiver crackles with static. "Base to Alpha Team," Wren says from back in Seattle.

"Whiskey here," West says. "What is it, Base?"

I touch Wyatt's arm. "Whiskey?"

"Code names," he says quietly. "Romeo—that's Ry—doesn't

use real names in the field. So West is Whiskey. Inara's Indigo. Graham is Golf."

"Hotel got another email. Sending it to you now."

My stomach flips. Simon's getting impatient. I don't want to see it. I can't watch Bettina suffer again. "Wyatt..." My voice cracks, and he wraps his arms around me.

"I'm right here, darlin'. I've got you."

Ripper angles his laptop while the rest of the team forms a protective semicircle around us. Do they know how alone I feel? How terrified I am?

Hope, it has been eight hours and you continue to try my patience. Return to me with what you stole, and perhaps I will be lenient with your punishment.

Three photos accompany the email. My legs give out at the sight of my friend—the only woman who dared speak to me for three years—sitting against a concrete wall. Bettina's arms are bound behind her, and she stares up at the camera. One eye is completely swollen, but the other is so wide, her terror bleeds through the screen. The front of her uniform dress is torn, exposing her bra. Angry red welts cover her chest, and her neck is so bruised, it's nearly purple.

I clutch Wyatt's black, long-sleeved shirt to stop my fingers from shaking so badly. "That's one of the basement walls," I manage over my own fear. "Only Simon, Brix, and Rex are allowed down there."

West scribbles note on his tablet, then returns his focus to the screen. "Open the other one, Rip."

Oh, God.

The windowless room upstairs is completely bare, save for a thin mattress. No furniture. No blanket or pillow. No lamp.

"What the fuck?" Wyatt asks.

Swallowing hard, I peer up at him. "He's letting me know he can take *everything* away. There used to be a bed in there. A small dresser with clothes. A nightstand with a lamp. Sometimes a treadmill—since insisted I keep myself in shape, even when he locked me in there for days at a time."

Wyatt's low growl should reassure me. But when Ripper opens the last photo, any hope I had vanishes.

Our plane. Sitting at the private airfield forty-five minutes outside of town.

With each plan West drew up, my confidence faltered a little more. Now, it's shattered into dust. We can't win. Not going in blind. I need air. Need to see the stars. To feel the breeze on my cheeks before I can't anymore.

Shoving at Wyatt, I twist out of his embrace. Before I can take two steps, I slam into Ryker, and it's like hitting a brick wall. One that catches my elbow to stop me from falling.

"Hope—"

"Let me go." My voice sounds so small. So afraid. Because I am. As soon as he loosens his grip, I run for the back door. The yard is nothing but dirt, and I fall to my hands and knees. My breath saws in and out of my chest, each gasp harder and harder until the canopy of stars above starts to fade.

"Count to ten, darlin'." Wyatt. He kneels next to me, his quiet, deep voice prompting me. "One. Two..."

By five, I know I won't pass out. But I also know what comes next. He helps me to my feet, but I resist when he tries to guide me back inside. "No. I need a few minutes out here. By myself."

"I am *not* leaving you," he says sharply. "Not after what we just saw."

"You have to let me go." I stumble back, prepared to run—even though I know he'd catch me. "Going in blind? It's suicide. He knows I'm here. Probably knows I'm not alone. What if he has more men now? He's smart, Wyatt. And careful. He'll know who you are. He'll expect you to have friends. What if there are ten guys with guns? Or twenty? What then?"

"She's right." West slips out the back door, Ryker following on his heels. "The plane's untraceable, but nothing and no one

—not even with our resources—can make FAA records disappear completely. I'd bet money he doesn't know how many we are. Or who we are. But he knows we exist."

Wyatt stares at West like he just started speaking another language. "So you're just *giving up?*"

Ryker scans our surroundings. "Hell no. But we need a new plan. One you're definitely *not* going to like."

"No fucking way," Wyatt growls. "Over my dead body."

It takes me several seconds to figure out what's going on, but when I meet West's gaze, all the puzzle pieces fall into place. "You're sending me back to Simon."

"No. They're not. We're leaving. I'll drive us back to Seattle if I have to, and as soon as we pick up Murphy, we'll disappear." Wyatt reaches for my hand, but I dart to West's side.

"If we do that, Bettina's dead." The first prickling of tears burns my eyes, but I force them away. "I'll go," I say, peering up at West. "If you promise me one thing."

"I'm listening," the former SEAL says as Wyatt lunges for me. Ryker blocks him, throwing out one massive arm and catching him across the chest.

"You all walk away. Drop me off half a mile from the compound, and leave. Go back to Seattle where it's safe."

Wyatt lets loose with a string of obscenities until Ryker shoves him toward the house. "Back inside. Now. Everyone. We're too fucking exposed out here."

My heart breaks into a million jagged pieces when West shakes his head. "Abandoning you? Not gonna happen. No man —no *one*—left behind. Come on. We only get one shot at this and we're running out of time."

With each step, a little more of me goes numb. Simon will kill all of them. Because of me. And there's nothing I can do to stop him.

20

Wyatt

SITTING on the floor in the corner of the room, I glare at Ryker's back. He stands between me and Hope while West outlines the plan. Smart move. If I didn't think he'd lay me out flat, I'd throw Hope over my shoulder and run. The idea of sending her back to that asshole—even for five minutes—fills me with a sickening combination of rage and dread. Abandoning these men and women who claim we're family should be the last thing I want to do. But Hope comes first. Always.

"We need eyes and ears inside the compound," West says. "It's a safe bet none of our tech is going to work beyond those walls. Not unless we can figure out exactly what's so special about the phones Simon uses." He nods to Ripper, and the hacker holds up two small, black pieces of plastic, each the size of my thumb.

"These should be able to clone the signal. *If* we can get it close enough to one of his men. We'll need an hour to figure out how to counteract his jammers. Maybe two."

Two hours? There's no fucking way she's spending two hours with that asshole.

Ryker shoots me a look when I start to get to my feet. I promised him I'd listen, so I sink back down and rest my head against the wall.

Across the room, West clears his throat. "In twenty minutes, Hope will reply to Simon's last message and tell him where he can pick her up. How close to one of his special phones does the receiver need to be?"

"Eight feet," Ripper says. The strain to his voice sets me on edge. I'm not sure how much longer I can hold it together. Or how I'm supposed to let Hope go, knowing she could be trapped in that house for two hours.

Simon could kill her in minutes. Or spend the whole time beating the crap out of her.

"Hope, you'll have a GPS tracker with you. We'll lose the signal once you're inside the compound, but we'll get it back as soon as we can disable whatever tech he's using. Try to get him to take you to Bettina, and stay there."

"What if he doesn't let me?" she asks. "He's seen the plane. He'll want to know who brought me here." Her voice breaks, and I can't sit still any longer. I have to hold her. To protect her for as long as I'm able. Shouldering past Ryker, I wrap my arms around her from behind.

The way she melts against me? I love this woman. Nothing in my life has ever mattered more than keeping her safe. "The best lies have a grain of truth to them," I say, my lips close to her ear. "If he interrogates you, tell him I brought you here. That we fought because I wanted to kill him."

Hope turns in my arms, panic in her eyes. "But then he'll know you're coming!"

"He'll know *Wyatt's* coming," West says. "One man. Not a team of five."

"Six," I say, meeting his gaze over Hope's head. "We're six. I'm not staying in the van."

Ryker growls an oath, and West holds up his hand. "Yes, you are. We're headed into a shitshow with limited intel, and you're compromised." Before I can protest again, he slants a quick gaze to Ripper. Fuck.

Ry didn't want me and Hope in the van to protect us. He wanted us to stay with Ripper. The man's fighting his worst memories twenty-four-seven. He left Seattle—Cara and Charlie—for me. For Hope. The way his shoulders hunch, how he flinches whenever anyone comes near, and the constant tremble in his fingers? He's hurting. Maybe not physically, but in every other way possible.

Rip needs an anchor. Can I really let these men and women risk their lives while I sit by and do nothing to be that for him?

If Hope dies, my life is over.

"Ry? A minute?" I nod toward the kitchen, and he follows me while West continues going over the plan. "Don't shut me out on this."

Pain etches lines around his eyes, and he shakes his head. "I need you to stay with Rip. If anything goes wrong—if I don't come back—"

"Stop right there. You don't think I see it? How hard this is for him? He doesn't need *me*. He needs you. So does Wren. And the baby. I'm not the one who should stay in the van. You are."

Whatever Ryker was expecting me to say, that wasn't it. He rubs a hand over the top of his head and blows out a long, slow breath. "I don't stay in the van. Never have."

"But you've stayed in Seattle for six months. Because you know any mission could be your last. Yet you're here. Why? Because I just happened to be there when you crawled out from under a dead bush eight clicks from Hell."

"I told you. We're family," he says, keeping his voice low.

"So prove it." Arms crossed over my chest, I stare him down

—or up, as he has more than six inches on me. "Prove to me that you know what family means. Stay in the van with your brother, and when this is all over—whatever happens—go back home to your wife and baby."

"Fuckin' hell," he mutters. "West's plan—"

"West can alter the plan. But the orders have to come from you." I reach out and grasp his arm just below the elbow. "I need to be a part of this, Ry. No matter how hard it is. I'll keep my shit together. For Hope, I can do it."

"I need your word—no, your promise. And before you answer, I'm gonna tell you what that means to me. To all of us." His eyes take on a soft shimmer, and from the way his body tenses, this is serious shit. "Wren lost her brother. Before Russia. She'd raised Zion after their mom ran out on them when he was still a kid. Promises meant *everything* to them, and when Z died..." He shakes his head, and his hand goes to the back of his neck for a long moment. "Promises led her to me. So this team—all of us here and everyone in Boston—we agreed. You never make a promise unless you're damn sure you can keep it."

"I hate this plan. The last thing I want is to send Hope anywhere near that asshole. But I trust West—and you—so, I promise. I'll follow orders, and I won't lose control again."

His quick nod is all I get. But it's enough. When Ryker McCabe makes a decision, he never looks back.

Hope

I have to avert my eyes from the bathroom mirror in front of me. The marble countertop is cool under my palms, but dusty, and I pick out half a dozen fingerprints. Left behind by a construction crew that will never know we were here.

On the plane, Wyatt and I donned all-black outfits—courtesy of Cara—but I just changed back into the yoga pants and light purple blouse I was wearing this morning.

Wyatt calls my name, then knocks softly. "It's almost time, darlin'. Can I come in?"

Brushing the dust from my fingers, I take a deep breath. I have to tell him how I feel. In case this whole plan goes to hell and my worst fears come true.

The door creaks, the sound sad and lonely in this big, unfinished house. It's empty now. All the computers, comms equipment, sketches, and gear stowed away in two black vans.

"Hope." The single word carries so much pain. "You can still say no."

His stubble tickles my fingers as I frame his face and crush my lips to his. He backs me up until my ass hits the counter, then lifts me so I can wrap my legs around his waist.

This man is everything I've ever wanted. Strong. Gentle. Kind.

The hard length pressed my mound makes me want more, and I wish we had time.

Not just for sex—though I crave the release and the connection we've found together—but for everything. Time for quiet breakfasts at home. Time for long walks with Murphy. Time to get to know each other's histories, hopes, and dreams.

Time to *live*.

Pulling back just far enough to meet his dark gaze, I whisper, "I'm scared."

Wyatt tightens his arms around me. I know he'd stop this if I asked. Even though we'd never be safe—or free—for the rest of our lives. He'd do it without question.

"Two hours, darlin'. After that, you'll never have to be afraid of him again."

If I live that long. If Ripper's little cloning device works. If I can do my part.

Only a week ago, Simon had his hands around my throat. Last month, he beat me so badly, I could barely walk for two days. West's plan depends on me being conscious and able to move.

"Let's go!" Ryker says from the hall. "We need to wipe that room down and get moving."

Wyatt eases me back onto my feet, then takes my hand. Our fingers twine. It's such a simple gesture, yet it means everything to me.

"Wren's sending the email now. Raelynn's in place, and Graham's waiting for Hope outside." Ryker's intense stare stops me in my tracks. My heart thuds against my chest like it's staging a jail break. "Remember the plan. No matter what happens, know we're coming for you."

No matter what happens.

I want to believe him. But he doesn't know Simon. Deep down, I'm terrified this is the last time I'll ever see Wyatt.

In the entryway, I throw my arms around his neck. "You're the best man I've ever met, Wyatt Blake. I..."

I can't get the words out. So instead, I hold on to him until I can't anymore. Until Ry tells me it's time to go.

Halfway to the taxi someone "borrowed" half an hour ago, I find my voice, but when I turn around, Wyatt's already closed the door.

THE CAB ROLLS to a stop across the street from a small park. At the other end of the block, a sleek, black sedan idles. Simon's men. Waiting for me. To take me back to my worst nightmare.

Graham turns in the driver's seat, and I pass him the twenty dollar bill I've had crushed in my grip the whole ride. Just in case we're being watched. "We're coming for you."

"Protect him. Please," I whisper. "And hurry."

Clutching my purse to my chest, I try not to hyperventilate as Graham drives away.

You can do this. Pain is temporary. In two hours...

Simon's men get out of the car—two of them—and wait for me. Orson and Rudy. Shit. They were friends with Brix. And from the way they look at me, they know I'm the reason he's dead.

Orson rips my purse from my hands so quickly, I stumble and crash into him. "You won't need that anymore." He shoves me at Rudy, and the shorter man grabs my arms hard enough I cry out.

"Everythin' okay here?" The breathless, Texas twang surprises Rudy, and he shifts me behind him. "I'm talkin' to the pretty little gal in the purple, dickface. Not you."

"I-I'm fine," I say. "Twisted my ankle. Rudy caught me."

Raelynn jams one hand on her hip and marches right up to the man. "Rudy, huh?" Popping an earbud from her ear, she glares up at him. Dressed in a pair of neon pink spandex pants and a University of Utah running shirt, she looks like any other student out for a run. This time of night, she can even pass for mid-twenties. "And what about you, sugar?" She trails a finger down Orson's chest. "Big strong men bein' so sweet to a gal with a bad ankle are men I think I should know. Too few of y'all in this town."

"That's Orson," I volunteer. "Thanks for...uh...checking on me. I'm fine. Really."

"And we have to get her home," Rudy says. "Now."

"Well, if y'all are good, I still got ten miles on my run, so..." Raelynn glances down at her sneakers, then huffs. "Well, will you look at that. Laces everywhere. Excuse me for two shakes. Gotta make sure I don't fall on my face."

After several long moments with Rudy's hand around my bicep and Orson crowding so close to me, all I can smell is the disgusting mix of his cologne and body odor, Raelynn pops back up. “Trainin’ for a marathon next month. Middle of the night is the best time to run.”

The men don’t say a word. She shrugs and gives me a little wave. “Breakfast is gonna taste so good in two hours. See ya’ around, sugar.”

And then she’s off.

Two hours.

She got what she needed. Or Ripper did.

Rudy shoves me into the back seat of the car. My hands skid on the leather. Before I can sit up, he’s right there, his hand on my neck. “Boss says, ‘Welcome home.’”

Thick fingers dig into the soft part of my shoulder. White hot agony consumes my entire body. I try to scream. The sound is nothing but a choked whimper. And then it stops.

Rudy jerks me upright. “Try anything, and I can make it a hundred times worse.”

Behind the wheel, Orson chuckles. “Enjoy your last car ride, bitch. You’ll be sorry for what happened to Brix, Matteo, and Tommy.”

“Don’t forget Preston,” Rudy says. His grip on my arm tightens. “He owed me two grand. Boss says I can collect when he’s done with you.”

I risk a quick glance at him and immediately regret it. I’m going to die. But not before they destroy me.

21

Hope

THE OUTER GATE LUMBERS OPEN, and two armed men stand just inside. Orson pulls out his phone and taps the screen half a dozen times before the guards move out of the way.

The semi-darkness of the garage ratchets up my anxiety another thousand notches. How much faster can my heart beat before it gives out? Rex stands at the door to the courtyard, arms crossed over his chest.

He and Brix were close. Only two years apart.

Rudy drags me out of the car, then shoves me at Rex. "Make sure there's still enough of her left for me to play with when you and the boss are done."

"Welcome home, princess." He twists my arm behind my back, trapping me against him. "I hope your little *trip* was worth what comes next."

His free hand gropes my ass, and my stomach flips. No. I can't let him touch me like that. I won't.

I bring my knee up as hard as I can, right into his balls. Rex doubles over with a groan. Running away won't do me any good. Not with Orson and Rudy right behind me. So I side-step Rex and race into the courtyard.

If I'm going to face Simon, I'm doing it on my terms. Or at least on my feet.

He's waiting in the formal living room. Along with four armed men I don't know. The head of the Salt Lake City brothel, Kyle, stands right behind him.

Rex is right on my heels. Before I can say a word, he kicks the back of my left knee, and I go down.

"That was uncalled for." Simon's tone is so mild, it terrifies me. "Hope, my sweet, please get up."

"Boss—"

Simon shoots Rex a look, and the big man mutters an apology—not to me but to Simon—under his breath.

My leg threatens to buckle, but I manage to stand on the second try.

"That is better." With his hands clasped behind his back, Simon approaches and looks me up and down. "Your hair is atrocious. And those clothes? Really, Hope. I thought I'd taught you better than that." With a curl to his lips, he grabs the hoodie and rips it down my arms. The motion sends me spinning. Right into Rex. "Check her!"

Rex molds his hands to my breasts, squeezing so hard, I gasp. The scent of wintergreen is overwhelming as he explores my body, dragging his hands down my stomach, over my hips, and between my legs.

"No wires or weapons," he says, and thank God he steps back.

Kyle, taller than Simon by a few inches, picks up a large, black wand. After a short beep, he waves it from my head to my shoes. "No tech either, boss."

Nothing you can find, jerk.

"At least you did something right. Now, where is the memory card?" Simon asks.

"In m-my purse," I say quietly, staring down at his perfectly polished loafers. He's too calm. Too cold. How long has it been? Twenty minutes? If I can talk to him, maybe he won't hurt me too badly before Wyatt and the rest of the team can get here.

Orson, who's leaning against the door to the courtyard, rips the pretty blue canvas bag in half. Tears prick at my eyes. I loved that bag. Even if I'd only had it for two days.

A pack of tissues, my lipstick, and my compact fall to the floor. There was no way I was bringing my wallet. Not when my ID still has my name as Hope Hastings.

"Nothing, boss," Orson says.

"Inside pocket," I add quickly. "In a little plastic case. It's all there. Everything I copied. You can get the investigation stopped. I know you can. Then everything can go back to the way it was. I did what you wanted. Let Bettina go. Please."

Simon laughs so hard, he doubles over, hands on his hips. "Let her...go? You stupid, naive bitch. I own her. I own *both* of you." He straightens, and all the amusement vanishes from his face.

Fear crawls up my throat, bitter on my tongue.

"Take my *property* to the basement," he says with a wave of his hand at Rex. "And make certain she's comfortable. I'll be down soon."

Kyle and Rex each grab one of my arms. My knee throbs. I can't keep my feet under me. "Simon! Please! I came back—"

Rex's punch steals my breath. I choke and gasp for air until pain sings along my right shoulder. I'm being dragged now. Sliding along the travertine. Kyle jerks my wrist—hard—and something pops.

Beeping.

I force my head up, squinting through the pain. Rex is tapping numbers on an electronic keypad, but it's too far away for me to make them out. That lock wasn't there a week ago.

Shit. What else changed? What if everything I told West is wrong now?

I try to scramble to my feet, but Rex has the door open too quickly. A set of concrete stairs disappears into darkness.

Kyle drops my arm, and I cradle it to my chest and curl into a ball. Until a rough hand snags my ankle.

"No! Don't!" I beg.

But Rex doesn't let go. My skull hits the second step so hard, I see stars.

"Protect your head, neck, and throat. Most vulnerable areas. For a woman, anyway."

West's advice echoes in my ears. Throwing my arms up to cradle my head, I clench my teeth. Can't scream. That's what they want.

Each step hurts worse than the last. My wrists. My back. My elbows.

How many more?

My arms go limp. All of me goes limp. Another crack to my skull, and I stop struggling against the darkness.

Wyatt, I love you. Hurry.

Wyatt

The clock is moving backwards. It's the only explanation for why we're still sitting here. In a van with blacked-out windows parked a full mile and a half from the compound, with no plan or way of knowing if Hope is all right. Or even still alive.

"You're positive?" Ry asks. "Because if that fuck stick doesn't give the performance of his goddamn life, I'm going to find him and flay the skin from his sack with a rusty vegetable peeler."

"That ain't the visual I needed before breakfast," Connor drawls over the small speaker in the center of the van's workspace. The former FBI agent retired a month ago, but still has enough contacts he trusts at the Bureau to figure out who the hell leaked word of the investigation to Simon. "Michaels knows if he don't fix what he broke, he's goin' away for the rest of his pitiful life, which in Gen Pop will last for approximately zero-point-two seconds."

Ryker scrubs both hands over his scarred head. "I owe you one. We all do."

"You don't owe me shit. We're family, remember? Tell Graham we're comin' out to Seattle for spring break. Finalized the dates with Q last night."

"He's a little busy right now, but he gave you a thumbs up. Gotta go, but anything changes, you know how to reach me." Ry ends the call and sinks into one of the bucket seats. "Fucking piece of shit junior agent couldn't resist a fifty grand bonus check."

The urge to hit something grows with every passing second. Thirty-seven minutes since two of Arrens' generals shoved Hope into the back of a car and drove away. The park was less than ten minutes from the compound. He's had twenty-nine minutes to hurt her. To terrorize her.

"Wyatt, focus up." West snaps his fingers, and I blink, hard. "You're going with Graham and Raelynn. We can't risk getting any closer with the van, and until we can make sure Arrens hasn't tapped into the local traffic camera network, hoofing it won't be quick. Grab your gear and stay hidden."

Graham passes me the smallest earbud I've ever seen. "Bone conduction. Make sure it fits. We have a couple different sizes."

It beeps softly once it's in. "Yankee, you copy?" West asks.

Slinging a black backpack over my shoulder, I wince as the strap tugs at the still-healing bullet wound from my last run-in with Simon's men. "Some reason I can't be Bravo?"

"Yeah. Because I said so. Get a move on."

It's a damn good thing West is my oldest friend. I shoot him a quick glare, then follow Graham and Raelynn—Golf and Sierra, since Ryker has a lock on Romeo—into the night.

The street is deserted at 3:00 a.m. Or maybe that's an illusion since we shot out the three closest street lights when we got here. Graham leads the way, Raelynn behind me.

No one speaks until we're in position. The soft green glow of my watch shouldn't be visible by anyone more than two feet away, so I risk a glance. Fuck. Fifty-three minutes.

"Golf, Sierra, and Yankee locked," Graham says over comms.

"Indigo in position." Inara is perched on a roof five hundred meters from the compound. Close enough she can cover the distance at a dead run in under two minutes—even with her rifle—but far enough away, she *should* be invisible.

"Whiskey locked. Alpha team? Status report." With West, all five of us are ready and waiting for Ripper and Wren to work their magic.

"Still working." The strain in Rip's voice doesn't reassure me. "Bastard paid a fucking fortune for this system."

I can't just sit behind this hedge—pine cones digging into my ass—and let Simon hurt the woman I love. "How much longer?"

"As long as it fucking takes," Ripper snaps. "Romeo's keeping an eye on things with the drone. We'll see anyone coming or going."

It's not enough. It'll never be enough. Not until Hope is safe in my arms again.

22

Hope

My neck aches. I try to reach up to touch it, but my arm won't move. Each beat of my heart throbs all the way to my eardrums. Not good.

Pain prickles along the back of my scalp as someone wrenches my head back—or up. Simon's face blurs in and out of focus. Can't see his eyes. Need to see his eyes. Need to know how angry he is. How much he'll hurt me.

"Nap time is over, Hope. Who brought you back to Salt Lake City and where are they now?"

I'm so dizzy. Tugging at my left hand does nothing. The right is half numb. Squinting, I think...shit. My wrists are zip tied to the arms of a metal chair.

"I need an answer."

Answer? I don't remember the question. It's harder than it should be to lift my gaze to his. "Huh?"

"Rex, please remind Hope of the rules."

Rules? What rules?

Fingers dig into both sides of my jaw, right under my ears.

Weak, gasping breaths are all I can manage. A spiderweb of agony covers my entire face and trails down my neck.

"Huuuurrts."

Simon leans close enough even my blurry vision isn't enough to hide the rage in his eyes. With a jerk of his hand, he tells Rex to stop, and my head lolls forward.

He grabs me by the chin. "Who was on that plane with you? I know you couldn't afford to charter a private flight here by yourself. You had no money. Nothing. So who is he?"

"The best lies have a grain of truth to them."

"Wyatt," I whisper. "His name is Wyatt."

My answer must please Simon, because he pats my cheek gently. "So it is him. The man who killed Brix, Matteo, Preston, and Tommy. Wyatt Blake. Former Navy SEAL. Retired with a Purple Heart and the Navy Medal of Honor."

He knows.

"Where is Mr. Blake now?" Simon asks.

How long has it been? The last thing I remember is falling —being dragged—down the stairs. I must have passed out. That's how they got me into this chair. But after that? I can't give up Wyatt's location if I haven't been here an hour. Ripper needs time to work.

I shake my head—big mistake. The room takes on a shimmer as a thousand stars explode in my vision. It's so bright, it hurts. Or maybe that's just the head injury.

Rex digs his knuckles into twin points just above each of my breasts. My scream echoes off the walls until I run out of air. He lets up for only a second, then starts in on me again.

Tears stream down my cheeks. My nose is running. Everything hurts. I writhe, desperate to get away, but the zip ties are too tight.

"Enough." Simon pulls out a handkerchief from his pocket and swipes at my face. "Disgusting. I can't stand to look at you in this state."

"Then...don't. Where's...Bettina?" I have to stall. Otherwise, I might not survive.

With an eye roll, Simon steps back and tosses the handkerchief on the floor. "Tell me where Mr. Blake is now, and I will let you see that pitiful excuse for a maid. Keep fighting me, and Rex will move on to the more *painful* pressure points."

More painful?

"The Grove Motel." I hang my head, like I can't believe I just gave up the man I love. "He...didn't want me to go. I snuck out."

"What room?"

My silence earns me what feels like an eternity of pure agony. Rex. His thick fingers just below my throat. Digging into —under?—my collar bones.

"Room...room thirty...one." Did I say that out loud? I must have. The pain starts to fade. I can't smell Rex's too-fresh breath.

Simon nudges my chin up. Narrowed eyes regard me with a mix of suspicion and curiosity. "Now we are getting somewhere. Does he know where I live?"

I manage a short nod. Got to distract Simon. Make him think what the team *wants* him to think. "He'll kill you."

His laugh sends a shiver down my spine as he turns his gaze to Rex.

"Send Rudy and Orson to the motel. Chad too. Put an end to this too-stupid-to-live Neanderthal and bring his body back here. Hope should be able to say goodbye to her lover."

"Simon, don't!" I cry. Leaning as far forward as I can, I pray he's as predictable as West hoped. "You don't need to do this. He'll never get to you. Not with all your security. He's harmless!" I don't have to fake my tears. Every one of my nerves feels like it's on fire, and the more I struggle against the zip ties, the more my wrists and ankles burn.

"No one who knows my name is harmless," Simon snarls. His hand flies, catching me across the cheek. The taste of copper fills my mouth. "You cost me millions in bribes. I almost lost *everything* because of you."

He's pacing now, back and forth so quickly, I can't follow him. It's too hard.

"I got the FBI investigation shut down—that was another two million by the time I was done—but all the businesses you used to hide my money over the past three years have been red flagged." He mops his brow with a fresh handkerchief.

I've never seen him this out of control. This Simon could do *anything*. Snap and kill me in seconds. Give me to Rex or Kyle or Orson and tell them to do their worst. Slit Bettina's throat just for fun.

He snaps his fingers, and I jerk. Rex and Kyle flank my chair. Each grab an arm—mine, of course, so it hurts more—spin me around, and shove the chair up to a folding table.

I lift my gaze, and suddenly it doesn't matter how much pain Simon causes me. Because ten feet in front of me, Bettina lies on the floor. Her chest stutters with each breath. Fresh scratches, bruises, and—oh my God—cigarette burns line her inner thighs. Her short uniform dress is ripped open all the way from her neck down to the hem, and though she tried to cover herself, I don't think she's wearing panties.

"Bettina!" I whip my head around, searching for Simon. Fuck. I'm so dizzy now, I want to throw up. "What did you do, you bastard?"

He swoops in from my left side. "I promised you she'd suffer." His thin lips curve into a smile, and too late, I start to suck in a deep breath. I know what's coming.

Simon wraps one hand around my throat, squeezing so hard, I can't get any air.

My arms and legs jerk violently, desperate to break free, but the plastic ties are too strong. *Simon* is too strong.

Burning. My chest. Lungs. Prickling pain in my eyes. Can't think. Air. Need air.

Please.

Simon's stare bores into me. Spasms rack my entire body. He's so angry. No control.

"Boss!" Rex shouts, and Simon jerks his hand away.

He's saying something. Lots of somethings. But all I hear over my own heartbeat is unintelligible ranting. Across from me, Bettina struggles to move. What is she doing?

Deep, heaving breaths leave me exhausted. I barely have the energy to keep my head up. More shouting. Rex. Simon.

"Not until we find the SEAL!" Rex says, getting right in Simon's face. "This is your fucking plan, boss. Stick to it!"

Simon pulls out his phone and jabs the screen. "Fine. Get the laptop. I'm unlocking the internet."

The internet. Why?

Rex places a sleek, black computer in front of me, opens it, and presses his index finger to the sensor.

"Simon?" I peer up at him, confused. Bettina manages to sit up, but the motion exposes more of her torso. I doubt there's even an inch that isn't bruised.

"You are going to fix your *mistakes*, my dear, sweet Hope." He reaches into his pocket for a folded piece of paper. "This is a list of clean companies. Ones the FBI haven't flagged. You will distribute my assets among these nine entities, and you will do it before the sun comes up."

"I c-can't. My head..."

The punch comes out of nowhere. Hard and fast and right to my jaw. Blood fills my mouth. Too much. Spitting it onto the floor, I struggle not to pass out.

"This is your last warning," Simon snarls.

When he curls his lip, he looks like a demented clown, and the thought almost makes me laugh. Until Rex stalks over to Bettina, kicks her, and presses his boot to her throat.

Simon fists my hair and forces me to meet his gaze. "I'd let my men have their fun with you until there was nothing left, but finding another accountant I can control will take me weeks. Do your job, or your pretty friend dies."

"I need...my hands," I whimper. "And...time. It's hard to think. Stairs...my head hurts so much. Please, Simon. Don't... hurt her."

"One hand," he snaps. "And you have three hours." Before he straightens, he twists my hair so hard, I cry out. "Rex will make sure you don't do anything you're not supposed to. All the bank logins are on that paper. Go anywhere else online, and Bettina loses an eye."

Rex pulls out a switchblade. It snaps open inches from Bettina's face. Her hoarse whimper brings a fresh round of tears. She squeezes her eyes shut when he traces a line from her lips all the way up her cheek, but thank God there's no blood.

"Be good, my sweet Hope." Simon heads for the stairs, and Rex slips the blade under the zip tie around my right wrist. He's not careful. When the plastic snaps in two, blood slicks my skin.

Asshole.

I need a distraction. If I can get Rex to leave the room, maybe we'll all make it out of this alive. If not...maybe I can at least find a way to get a message to the team.

Wyatt

"Got movement," Ry says, his deep voice somehow even rougher over comms. "Three men in a black sedan. The two assholes from the park and another."

"Base to Alpha Team." Wren. It's five in the morning here. An hour earlier in Seattle. I cringe, still hiding behind a tall hedge. Ry's gonna be pissed.

"Base, you should be offline."

Yep. Called it.

"Third man is one Chad Ravens. Two arrests for harassment, both charges were dismissed, and a third for stalking. That one is still open."

"Where the fuck did he come from? He wasn't on the list. And why are you awake?"

"Because *someone* won't stop kicking my bladder," Wren retorts. "And because you're on mission. If you think I'm *ever* going to sleep when you're out there—"

"Cut the chatter. Both of you. Romeo, get in position. They'll be at the motel in five minutes," West mutters. "Charlie, what's your status?"

Charlie? Shit. Rip's dog. Of course he'd pick that for his code name.

"Close. I think. When we're back, we're going through this code line by line. We can use this tech. Base, I need your help with these last couple of functions."

"You got it, Charlie," Wren says. "Send it ov—fudgenuggets!"

I tense, sitting up straighter and flexing my screaming muscles. Wren doesn't swear. Fudgenuggets is serious.

"Base?" Ry asks. "Report!"

"I have a way in. Yankee? Hotel's alive. She's transferring money from the companies the FBI red flagged to half a dozen other accounts. From inside the target zone." Wren's so excited, her words are falling all over one another. "Each transfer has a three- or four-letter code attached to it, and I think...hang on."

Thirty seconds. Sixty. Ninety. Fuck. How long until I lose my shit and demand an update?

Do not yell at the pregnant woman working her ass off for you and Hope. You're not that much of an asshole. Remember?

"Base to Alpha Team. She is definitely sending us a message. So far, it reads: 'Basement. RD. Internet open.' Charlie, keep working. I'm going to send a spike to Arrens' computer and see if I can take down the whole system. Without knowing anything about his firewalls, this could be quick, or it could take an hour. But at least we have a backup plan. Base out."

"Dumbasses neutralized," Ry says quietly. "No resistance. Sent confirmation of Yankee's death to the Target via text. You'd better be close, Charlie. He'll expect these three back in fifteen minutes."

"I am." There's a quiet confidence in Ripper's tone that wasn't there before.

We're getting Hope back. And Simon Arrens is going to die for what he's done. To her and everyone else he's ever hurt.

23

Hope

TWO HOURS AND TWENTY-SEVEN MINUTES. Where are they?

Rex hasn't left me alone or turned his back the whole time, and I'm terrified he's going to notice the codes I'm attaching to each transfer. Or that I'll forget what letters to use next.

My head feels like someone's using it for basketball practice. Hell, there isn't a single part of me that doesn't hurt.

"I need water," I croak. It's not a lie. I'm parched.

"When you're done." He jams two fingers down on my left wrist—along the bone—and I yelp. My vision goes white from the pain.

"Can't finish...with you...doing...that..."

The pressure eases. "Whiny little bitch," he says under his breath.

"Asshole," Bettina hisses. Sitting up against the wall, she looks so frail. But fire burns in her brown eyes. "*Eres tan feo que hiciste llorar a una cebolla.*"

A laugh bubbles up in my throat until Rex growls something unintelligible and stalks over to her. Shit. Stop him? Or use the distraction?

"Is that the best you can do?" he snarls. "I'm so ugly I make an onion cry? I can make you that ugly in seconds!"

She screams and kicks at him, catching him in the ankle.

Now. Move, now, Hope.

It's awkward as hell to reach down to my right foot, but as Rex kicks Bettina in the hip, I dig into my shoe. The narrow, serrated file West slipped under the insole isn't enough of a weapon for me to overpower Rex, but it'll get me out of these zip ties. If I have enough time to use it.

Bettina's whimpers put an end to that plan too soon. I can't let him keep hurting her. Sliding the file up my left sleeve, I call his name.

"Stop! Or the next transfer I make will send a million dollars directly to the federal government." He won't understand there's no way I can actually *do* that. The threat is effective enough. Rex shoves Bettina to the floor.

"If you try anything..." he warns, stalking back to my side.

"I know. More pain. You're so creative." The slap sends my head whipping to the side.

Shut up, Hope. Just a little longer and Wyatt will come for you.

The laptop screen flickers. Huh? The code I'd entered on this transfer, *nin30*, letting someone—Wren, I hope—know that Simon's due back in the basement in thirty minutes, changes.

In10.

Ten minutes? They're going to be here in ten minutes? I can hold out for ten more minutes. I have to.

Another flicker, and the code disappears. Quickly, I add *OK* to the transfer note, then send it off. Four accounts left, and now...nine minutes. Curling the fingers of my left hand, I close them around the tip of the file.

They're coming for me. I have to be ready.

Wyatt

"In position to cut the power." West's words in my ear are the best fucking thing I've heard all day. We've been in position for over an hour and a half. Any longer, and I was going over the wall on my own, damn any consequences.

"Base, you good to go?" Rip asks.

"Base is ready. Count it down, Charlie."

The brief silence is long enough for me to close my eyes and visualize my target. The south wall of the compound. Twelve feet up and over. A drop onto grass. Then fifty feet to the front door. Thermals better fucking work or we're breaching the house blind.

"On my mark," Rip says quietly. "Three. Two. One. Go."

The floodlights illuminating the outer wall flicker—Wren's infiltration of Simon's network—and someone shouts. "What the hell was that?"

I take off at a dead run, covering the distance in under a minute. The wall looms tall above me. The instant everything goes dark, I throw the small grappling hook up and over the wall. It lands with a quiet *plink*, catches, and I start to climb.

The power comes back on with a dull hum of equipment, lights, and a blaring alarm from inside the house. "Yankee. Eight o'clock," Ry says in my ear. Spinning around, I fire a single shot from my silenced MK-23. It finds its mark in a tall, black-clad man's neck, and he goes down.

"Three heat signatures in the basement, two more heading that direction. Breach!"

Thank fuck Ryker agreed to stay in the van. He's calm in a way I could never be. Not with Hope's life at stake. Glass shatters to the east, and I break down the front door with a hard kick. Asshole was so confident in his security, he didn't bother to reinforce the lock.

Raelynn sweeps into the great room from the north. "Clear. On your six, Yankee."

"Multiple hostiles in and around the garage." This from Graham. "I count eight."

"Five now," Inara says. "On my way."

The door to the basement doesn't budge, even when I give it a second and third kick. "Out of the way," Raelynn hisses. I turn to argue, until I see the det cord coiled in her gloved fingers.

Thirty seconds later, we retreat behind the wall of Simon's office. She tugs at her black knit cap, then pulls out the detonator.

"Fire in the—" Bits of plaster pelt us as bullets land in the drywall between us. "Sheeiiit."

We drop and roll. The small, plastic control box slips from her hand. With one bad bounce on the marble floor, the cover pops off.

No!

I need to get to the basement. Right fucking now. "Cover me!"

She fires—a good six shots—but whoever's on the other side of the wall must be weaving, because we're still pinned down behind a heavy oak desk taking hits every few seconds.

The detonator pieces almost slip from my hands. I have to get my shit together. Hope's life depends on it. "Need an assist," Raelynn says. "South-east corner office."

West answers, "Two minutes."

That's ninety seconds too long. "Romeo?" I ask. The detonator's toast. I'll have to blow the door the hard way.

My watch buzzes, and I glance down at the screen. I've never been so thankful for tech in my entire fucking life. The thermal scan of the great room on the other side of the wall shows two hostiles in constant motion.

Raelynn gives me a wicked smile. "Like shootin' fish in a barrel." Bracing her right hand on her left forearm, she tracks their movements. "Get ready to move."

I nod, crouched like I'm about to compete in the fifty-yard-dash. After two shots, I take off. A guy in a black t-shirt and khaki pants races down the stairs, and I drop him with two shots, center mass.

Should have worn body armor, asshole.

Pressing myself against the wall twenty feet from the basement door, I take aim. "Romeo? Am I clear?"

"Clear."

The entire door pops off its hinges with one shot to the det cord. It teeters for a split second, then hits the floor with a massive *crack*.

Another buzz on my wrist, and I'm looking at the scan of the basement. It's grainy, the cement walls interfering with the signal. But all the heat signatures are close together.

"Give it up, asswipe!" I shout. "Send Hope and Bettina up the stairs, and maybe we'll let you live!"

Hope's choked scream nearly sends me to my knees. Arrens is hurting her, and nothing—not even a set of stairs with zero cover—is going to keep me away from her a moment longer.

"Don't be a damn fool," Raelynn says as she hits wall next to me. Another cry, this one weaker, and I glare at her. "We're gettin' her back. But we ain't fixin' to charge down there like someone jerked a knot in our tail."

"If it were the love of your life down there—"

Her blue eyes harden, and she reaches into the pocket of her tactical vest. "The love of my life died in my arms. Bring him up again, and I'll break my foot off in your ass." She pulls the pin on the flash bang and shouts, "Hope y'all have sunscreen!"

The stun grenade hits the stairs, and we both cover our ears and squeeze our eyes shut. Even from thirty feet away, I can feel the blast. When the sound fades, I fly down the stairs at a dead run, praying Hope at least had time to close her eyes.

Kyle's sprawled on the floor at the bottom of the stairs, only inches from the spent grenade, not moving. A folding table's on its side across the room. Where the fuck is Hope?

A shot hits me in the shoulder—my bad shoulder—and my knees slam into the concrete. The MK-23 slips from my hand.

"Wyatt! No!"

Hope.

My lungs are screaming, but the impact short-circuited my diaphragm, and I can't even draw a shallow breath. Arrens rises from behind the table, laughing, and Rex yanks Hope against him.

She's alive. Bruised. Terrified. Disoriented. But alive.

Shots hit the wall behind them. Simon fires back, and Raelynn calls for backup. Something's wrong with her voice. Is she hit?

Rolling onto my side, I manage to suck in a wheezing breath. Backup won't do shit.

Hope's eyes are glassy, and from the way her arms are pinned behind her, she's restrained somehow. Rex grips the back of her neck, fingers and thumb digging into either side of her jaw just under her ears.

Her keening cry is pure agony, and I think she's only standing because his grip is so strong.

"Say goodbye to your lover, Hope." Simon aims a Glock 19 at my head.

This is it. I'm going to die. And so is she unless someone has a spare miracle lying around. "I love you, darlin'. I should have told you sooner. Every fucking minute of every day since we got to Seattle. Because that's when I knew."

Something shifts in Hope's eyes. The haze of pain clears, and she throws herself backwards against Rex. The man yelps. It's enough. One second of distraction. Simon's aim wavers. His gaze turns to Hope and his only remaining general.

Something metallic hits the ground. My fingers close around the grip of the MK-23, and I fire.

Arrens doesn't make a sound. The single shot to his head smokes, and his eyes roll around in their sockets. A stain darkens the front of his thousand-dollar pants. Before his bladder empties completely, he collapses.

"Hope!"

She catches her knee on the side of the table, and almost crashes down on top of me. Nothing is more important than holding her. Until she starts struggling in my arms.

"My hands..."

"Fuck. I'm sorry." Sitting up, I pull the knife from its sheath and snap the zip tie. "Are you hurt? What did he—"

"You fucking bitch!" Rex braces one hand on the upended table. Blood glistens all around the zipper of his khakis, but he's still got enough fight left in him—along with Simon's gun—to end both of us.

I'm about to shove Hope behind me when Bettina pushes to her feet just out of Rex's view. Something silvery glints in her hand.

I grin. "Might want to watch your mouth, shit-for-brains. You're the one who's fucked."

Death comes for Rex wearing a torn, gray dress. Bettina clutches the blade Hope used to stab him in the family jewels, and there's such fire in her eyes, I almost wish he could see it.

"Que te folle un pez!" she screams and drags the weapon across his carotid artery.

Rex drops the gun, his hands pressed to his throat, but he's already dead. He just doesn't know it yet. Hope buries her face in the crook of my neck, and I rub circles along her back until she whimpers quietly.

"You're hurt." Every protective bone in my body—which is

all of them where she's concerned—demands revenge, but the men who tortured her will never touch anyone ever again. "What did he do to you, darlin'? Tell me."

With a final gurgle, Rex breathes his last. Bettina staggers back until she hits the wall and stares at his body like she's waiting for his ghost to arise so she can kill it too.

"Yankee! What's your status?" West asks over comms. But a hint of his voice carries down the concrete steps, so I know he's close.

"We're clear. Get someone down here to help Bettina. I've got Hope." She's trembling now, and bite down on one finger of my glove to pull it off. I need to feel her, to touch her. The skin of her cheek is hot under my palm.

Ghosting my thumb along her jaw, I watch her eyes. She flinches when I reach the pressure point that pig fucker used. "How bad?"

"I'll...b-be okay. Just want to get out of here. Please?" Tears shimmer on her lashes. I'd give this woman the entire goddamn world if I could.

"That I can do." My shoulder protests every single movement, but I can ignore the pain. For Hope, I can do anything.

"Well, ain't this the prettiest sight." Raelynn holds her right arm tight to her body, her thumb hooked in a loop on her vest. From her expression, she's in a hell of a lot of pain, but I don't see any blood. "Sugar," she says, holding up her left hand as she approaches Bettina, "you can keep that blade, but let me help you upstairs, okay? We'll get you cleaned up and then we'll get the hell outta here."

"My sister." Bettina turns to Hope. "Carla is still trapped. I cannot leave without her!"

"We know all about her, sugar. Soon as we finish here, we're fixin' to shut down every one of the brothels. So come on, now. You'll be with Carla real soon."

The two women shuffle toward the stairs, passing Graham on his way down. "You hurt?" he asks us.

"I'm good. Hope needs a doctor."

"No." She clutches my vest, and I peer down at her. "I just need you."

We'll see about that. She might be the bravest—and most stubborn—woman I've ever met, but I'm not above carting her off to a doctor whether she wants it or not. There's nothing I won't do to keep her safe.

Nothing.

EPILOGUE

Hope

I DON'T REMEMBER MUCH after Wyatt practically carried me out of Simon's house. Ripper waiting for us in the van. A very painful climb up the stairs to the plane. Having to strip down to my bra and panties so West could make sure I didn't need a doctor.

The one thing I *do* remember? The worried look on Wyatt's face. It's still there. Even though the sun's up—it's almost 10:00 a.m.—we haven't slept. Thanks to Ryker's connections, half a dozen men and women stand guard around the plane in case any of the local police try to give us trouble.

I can't get comfortable. Every time I take a deep breath, something else hurts.

"You need a doctor," Wyatt says. "I don't care *what* West thinks. The minute we land, we're going to the hospital."

"I just want to go home." My fingers tremble as I touch his jaw. "Take me home, Wyatt. To that nice apartment with Cara and Ripper next door."

“Don’t forget Graham and Q on the other side.” He presses a gentle kiss to my forehead. “We’ll be back there soon.”

“Back home?” My head throbs, and I can’t figure out how to tell him I want to live in Seattle—with him—forever.

“Hope, what’s wrong?” Concern furrows his brow. “You know we’re going home.”

“I love you.” The words tumble from my lips as tears burn in the corners of my eyes. “I tried to tell you before. But I was so scared.”

Wyatt cups my cheeks gently and brushes his lips to mine. “I know, darlin’. Hardest thing I ever had to do was let you get into that cab. I wanted to toss you over my shoulder and run as far and as fast as we could. But I wanted you to be free even more.”

Free. The word bounces around in my head—my throbbing, fuzzy, aching head. Then I burst into tears. Every muscle aches. Down to my fingers and toes. Wyatt’s afraid to touch me, and if I’m honest, I’m scared too. But I need his arms around me.

“Hope? Fuck. You’re going to the hospital.” Wyatt glances around the plane like he’s desperate for *someone* to help him. To help me.

Sniffling, I swipe at my nose. “I need you to hold me. You won’t hurt me. Just...love me.”

Shoving the armrest up, he shifts in his seat and opens his arms. I settle against him, and though I was wrong—even the lightest pressure on my back is almost too much—I’m safe. Held by the man I love.

“They’re on their way,” Ripper says a few minutes later. He’s on his fiftieth trip up and down the aisle since West, Graham, Inara, and Ry left to shut down the brothel on the north side of the city. “Carla’s with them.”

“*Gracias a Dios.*” Across from us, Bettina covers her face with her hands, crying with relief, and I’d comfort her if I thought I could get up. Raelynn and Inara gave her fresh clothes, and she let West examine the worst of her burns, even though she sobbed the whole time.

"Y'all want coffee?" Raelynn asks. West ordered her to stay put after finding out she'd dislocated her shoulder fighting with one of Simon's goons—and then popped it back in herself five minutes later. Her duct tape sling earned her the field medic's side eye, but he couldn't argue with how well it worked.

"Oh, hell yes. Is there any food?" As if my stomach has only *now* realized I haven't eaten in more than eighteen hours, it growls loudly.

"We got a whole case of MREs. But unless you're hankerin' for the worst meal of your life, I wouldn't risk one." She putters around in the little kitchenette at the back of the plane for a few minutes, and the rich scent of dark roast fills the space.

"Found a little somethin' special." Raelynn sets a tray on the table in front of us. Four cups of coffee and two chocolate bars. "Don't tell Ryker I had those in my pack. I'd never hear the end of it." She winks at me, then nudges one of the bars toward Bettina. "Go on, sugar. Ain't no one gonna tell you what you can and can't eat ever again."

The look Bettina gives her? Pure joy. I don't care how hungry I am. There's no way I'm touching the other bar. Bettina deserves both of them.

Before she gets even halfway through the chocolate, Ripper clears his throat. "They're back."

"Carla?" Bettina pushes to her feet as the plane door opens. The sisters hold on to one another for so long, Inara has to guide them to a plush couch at the back of the plane so we can take off.

Ryker drops into one of the seats across from us. "Eighteen women. Six men. All under the age of twenty-five. All taken off the streets. Mexico. Canada. Panama."

"Where are they now?" Wyatt asks.

"With people I trust. In a few days, they can decide if they want to go back home or stay in the United States. Got half a dozen FBI agents on the way from the Austin field office. They'll show up tomorrow and clean up the rest of the mess that piece of shit left behind. And once we regroup at home, we'll hit all the other brothels that fuckstick ran and shut them down too." He drags a hand over his head, rubbing along one of the worst of the scars. "Not sure what it was about this one. But fuck. I'm glad it's over."

One Month Later

Wyatt

"We're here, darlin'." I shut off the engine and stare at the cabin. For three years, this was my home. But after four weeks in Seattle building a life with Hope, I wasn't sure I'd ever come back up here again.

Until I came home from a walk with Murphy and she had a suitcase open on the bed.

I panicked, terrified she was leaving me. That she'd come to her senses—despite how many times we've said "I love you" since we came back from Salt Lake City.

"Hope? What are you doing?"

She jumps, a nervous laugh escaping her lips. "I didn't think you'd be home for another half an hour."

"I missed you. I thought we could grab dinner at that Thai place on the corner." Murphy presses himself to my legs. He can feel my growing panic. "Are you...leaving?"

Hope drops the sweatshirt she was folding, her eyes wide. "Leaving? Wyatt, I love you."

"Then...why are you packing?" I'm not proud of the desperate

tone to my voice. We have a life here now. Friends. Family. Hope started taking on some small accounting jobs from home, and she and Ripper have been talking about how they can make Hidden Agenda's investments more profitable. The salary I earn working with Ry and his team is plenty to keep us going—since the man doesn't charge us a cent for this apartment—and we've bought clothes, dishes, throw pillows—even put up a few pieces of inexpensive art.

"Wyatt, look at the suitcase." Hope's expression is one hundred percent "I can't believe I have to explain this to you."

Flannel shirts. Levi's. My hiking boots. Cable-knit sweaters for her, leggings, wool caps, and thick gloves.

"You're packing for the cabin. But I thought we agreed..."

Reaching up to touch my cheek, she smiles. Her bruises have faded, and her sprained shoulder rarely bothers her anymore. "We agreed Seattle was home. Not to stay here three hundred-and-sixty-five days a year. Why can't we live here...but spend a week up in the mountains every month or so? You love it up there. And even though I don't ever want to live in a world without Netflix, Dinner Dash, and central heating, getting away from the city from time to time? It's something we both need. West...um...sort of wired it for satellite internet a few days ago. So we won't be totally cut off. Just...by ourselves."

It was the best damn gift anyone's ever given me. Understanding. Compromise. Love.

Hope stretches in the bucket seat. Ry let me take one of Hidden Agenda's trucks up here for the week. Both because we decided not to buy a car and because the four-wheel-drive vehicle comes with GPS tracking. I'm not complaining.

"Well, mountain man? You carried me inside the first time you brought me here. Want to do it again?"

Even after a month, Hope still has some pain. A hairline fracture to one of her vertebrae—being dragged down a set of stone steps isn't good for the spine—healed badly, and some days, she struggles.

"Be honest with me, darlin'," I say as I scoop her into my arms. Murphy runs ahead of us, circling the cabin so he can use his special doggie door to beat us inside. "What's today's number?"

"Only a two. It's a good day, Wyatt. I'm fine. I just wanted to wrap my arms around you after that long drive. And maybe..." she arches her brows in a way I'll never be able to resist, "convince you to carry me straight into the bedroom, strip me naked, and show me a little more of the mountain man's Kama Sutra. We only made a dent in it the last time, and you know me."

Nudging the door with my foot, I carry her over the threshold. I've seen that gleam in her eyes before. "I do, darlin'. You're an over-achiever."

"So...?"

The bed beckons. "So, we'd better get started. I want you at least twice before dinner."

"I love you, Wyatt. Come here, so I can show you just how much."

Peeling off my shirt, I don't even *think* about hiding from her. Hope accepts me. My scars. My occasional foot-in-mouth awkwardness. My intense and overwhelming need to protect her.

We've had some bad days. I've triggered her more than once. But our love survived a madman with more than a dozen men guarding his compound. There isn't anything we can't handle. Together.

THANK you for reading Defending His Hope. It's my greatest hope—ha—that you enjoyed this expanded version of the book as much as I enjoyed writing it. .

I hope you'll consider leaving a review wherever you

purchased Defending His Hope. Reviews—even short ones—are so important to your favorite authors. You don't have to write much. A single sentence or two about how the book made you feel is plenty! If you can leave a brief review, I'd appreciate it so very much.

The next book in the Away From Keyboard series is available for pre-order now! Trusting His Instincts is Raelynn's story. I can't tell you much about it yet, but trust me. It's gonna be smoking hot and full of Texas sass.

I hope you'll check out Trusting His Instincts!

As always, you can find out the latest information about all of my books and upcoming plans through my newsletter or my Unstoppable Forces reader group on Facebook!

ACKNOWLEDGMENTS

Defending His Hope would not be what it is without so many folks in my corner.

Lauren, thank you for always being a positive force in my world.

Jill, I'm so happy we finally got to meet after so many years of friendship. I'm even happier we found out we don't drive each other batty in person. Love you.

To my Avalon family, especially Nibs, Death, Scarlett, and Rielle, you are the best! Thanks for the last minute character names, and for the inspiration for one scene in particular.

Most of all, thank you to everyone who buys, reads, and reviews my books. You make every one of my days brighter.

ABOUT THE AUTHOR

Patricia D. Eddy writes romance for the beautifully broken. Fueled by coffee, wine, and Doctor Who episodes on repeat, she brings damaged heroes and heroines together to find their happy ever afters in many different worlds. From military to paranormal to BDSM, her characters are unstoppable forces colliding with such heat, sparks always fly.

Patricia makes her home in Seattle with her husband and very spoiled cats, and when she's not writing, she loves working on home improvement projects, especially if they involve power tools.

Her award-winning *Away From Keyboard* series will always be her first love, because that's where she realized the characters in her head were telling their own stories—and she was just writing them down.

You can reach Patricia all over the web...
patriciadeddy.com
patricia@patriciadeddy.com

facebook.com/patriciadeddyauthor
twitter.com/patriciadeddy
instagram.com/patriciadeddy
bookbub.com/profile/patricia-d-eddy
tiktok.com/@patriciadeddyauthor

ALSO BY PATRICIA D. EDDY

Away From Keyboard

Dive into a steamy mix of geekery and military prowess with the men and women of Hidden Agenda and Second Sight.

Breaking His Code

In Her Sights

On His Six

Second Sight

By Lethal Force

Fighting For Valor

Finding Their Forevers (a holiday short story)

Call Sign: Redemption

Braving His Past

Protecting His Target

Defending His Hope

Trusting His Instincts

Gone Rogue (an Away From Keyboard spinoff series)

Rogue Protector

Rogue Officer

Rogue Survivor

Rogue Defender

Dark PNR

These novellas will take you into the darker side of the paranormal with vampires, witches, angels, demons, and more.

Forever Kept

Immortal Hunter

Wicked Omens

Storm of Sin

By the Fates

Check out the COMPLETE By the Fates series if you love dark and steamy tales of witches, devils, and an epic battle between good and evil.

By the Fates, Freed

Destined: A By the Fates Story

By the Fates, Fought

By the Fates, Fulfilled

In Blood

If you love hot Italian vampires and and a human who can hold her own against beings far stronger, then the In Blood series is for you.

Secrets in Blood

Revelations in Blood

Holidays and Heroes

Beauty isn't only skin deep and not all scars heal. Come swoon over sexy vets and the men and women who love them.

Mistletoe and Mochas

Love and Libations

Restrained

Do you like to be tied up? Or read about characters who do? Enjoy a fresh COMPLETE BDSM series that will leave you begging for more.

In His Silks

Christmas Silks

All Tied Up For New Year's

In His Collar

CPSIA information can be obtained
at www.ICGtesting.com
Printed in the USA
BVHW031212110722
641843BV00012B/534

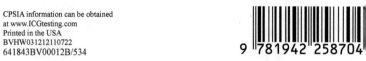

9 781942 258704